SEMIPRECIOUS

D. ANNE LOVE

MARGARET K. McELDERRY BOOKS

NEW YORK LONDON TORONTO SYDNEY

For my mother

MARGARET K. MCELDERRY BOOKS
An imprint of Simon & Schuster Children's Publishing Division
1230 Avenue of the Americas, New York, NY 10020
This book is a work of fiction. Any references to historical events, real people, or real locales are used fictitiously. Other names, characters, places, and incidents are the product of the author's imagination, and any resemblance to actual events or locales or persons, living or dead, is entirely coincidental.
Copyright © 2006 by D. Anne Love
MARGARET K. MCELDERRY BOOKS is a trademark of Simon & Schuster, Inc.
For information about special discounts for bulk purchases, please contact Simon & Schuster Special Sales at 1-866-506-1949 or business@simonandschuster.com.
The Simon & Schuster Speakers Bureau can bring authors to your live event. For more information or to book an event, contact the Simon & Schuster Speakers Bureau at 1-866-248-3049 or visit our website at www.simonspeakers.com.
Also available in a hardcover edition.
Book design by Christopher Grassi
The text for this book is set in Mrs. Eaves Roman.
Manufactured in the United States of America
First paperback edition October 2009
2 4 6 8 10 9 7 5 3 1
The Library of Congress has cataloged the hardcover edition as follows:
Love, D. Anne.
Semiprecious / D. Anne Love.—1st ed.
p. cm.
Summary: Uprooted and living with an aunt in 1960s Oklahoma, thirteen-year-old Garnet and her older sister, Opal, brave their mother's desertion and their father's recovery from an accident, learning that "the best home of all is the one you make inside yourself."
ISBN 978-0-689-85638-9 (hc)
1. Mothers and daughters—Fiction. [1. Family life—Oklahoma—Fiction. 2. Schools—Fiction. 3. Oklahoma—History—20th century—Fiction.] I. Title.
PZ7.L9549Sem 2006
[Fic]—dc22
2005014906
ISBN 978-0-689-87389-8 (pbk)
ISBN 978-1-4169-9696-5 (eBook)

ACKNOWLEDGMENTS

I'm hugely grateful for Desmond Rochfort's research and writing, which so eloquently explains the work of the Mexican muralists. I owe an even larger debt to Sarah Sevier for her unwavering enthusiasm, good humor, and patience. And finally, to my fellow writers in Austin, who were never too busy with their own work to ask how mine was going: Thanks, and Godspeed.

CHAPTER ONE

My name is Garnet Olivia Hubbard. In five weeks and three days, I'll be thirteen.

My sister Opal, who is fifteen and the self-appointed Boss of the Entire Universe, rolls her eyes every time I remind her I am about to become an honest-to-Pete teenager. She says I'm still a baby. If I'd called her a baby when *she* was thirteen, I'd still be recovering from my injuries. Anyway, it isn't true. I'm no baby. I've had to grow up fast, because of what happened on Mama's birthday last summer.

It was the first day of August, the last day of my regular life, and I didn't have a clue. Just before daylight I got up, unlatched the back door, and went to the garden. The tomato plants and Mama's pole beans were heavy with dew. Already the thermometer on the back porch was pushing ninety degrees, but I didn't mind the heat. I love summer, when there are no math quizzes or vocabulary lists. You can sleep as long as you want, then wake up to a clean slate where anything is possible, and you can make the day into whatever you want it to be. I wanted Mama's birthday to be perfect.

Deep in the corn rows the air was humid and still. I thumped the bugs off the corn, gathered four ears, and picked half a dozen tomatoes for the dinner Opal and I were making for Mama, a tradition as important as going to the opening game at the ballpark every spring, or staying up until midnight on Christmas Eve. The birds were waking up and singing their little hearts out. The morning freight train clattered through town bound for Dallas, its whistle echoing through the trees along Piney Road. At Mrs. Streeter's house next door, the screen door slapped open and her three-legged cat shot out and perched on the porch railing. Mrs. Streeter, in her nightgown and rhinestone-studded glasses, marched across the grass to fetch her copy of the Mirabeau *Daily Monitor*. She picked it up and waved to me on her way back inside.

Then the lamp in my room came on, a sign Opal was up, getting ready to bake Mama's cake. As for Mama herself, she was still out like a light, getting her beauty sleep so she'd be fresh for her party.

My daddy was on his way home for the celebration. He worked on a ship called the *World Explorer*. It was based in New Orleans but sailed all over the Gulf of Mexico looking for places to drill for oil and gas. Mama said it was dangerous work, but Daddy said the pay was good, and he liked being outside instead of behind a desk. The worst part of his job was his being gone so much. Already he'd missed my first baseball game of the season and Opal's portrayal of Juliet in the eighth-grade play, which had gotten written up on the entertainment page of the paper. Me and Opal had been mad at him for missing our important events, even though it wasn't his fault. When it came to Mama, he wasn't taking any chances on making her mad by missing her big day. He got permission to come home for her birthday, even though he'd have to turn right around the next morning and drive all the way back to New Orleans.

I cut some okra off the stalks and headed for the house. The screen door banged as I came in, and Opal said, "Shhh! Don't wake her up."

I shucked the corn, rinsed the tomatoes, and helped Opal make a double batch of chocolate frosting. When the cake was done, we set it on the rack to cool, then tiptoed past Mama's door to get cleaned up. Later, we made PB & J sandwiches and iced tea for lunch and ate on the back porch, then finished frosting the cake.

We heard Mama's door open and close, and then the squeak of the faucet in her shower. Opal cocked her ear, listening for the beginning of Mama's daily serenade. Occasionally Mama sang a gospel tune, but mostly she sang country. She claimed to know the words to every song ever played on her favorite station, WSM. Today, though, we didn't hear anything but the shower running and the banging of the old pipes.

By five o'clock we could hear Mama opening and closing drawers, moving around in her room, getting ready for her grand entrance. Opal gave up watching for Daddy and went to our room to play records. I was sitting in Daddy's easy chair by the window, reading *Black Beauty* for the umpteenth time, when I saw his pickup barreling down the road, kicking up a cloud of dust. I yelled for Mama and Opal and ran out the door to meet him.

"Hey, sugar pie!" Daddy unfolded himself from behind the wheel, scooped me up, and twirled me around. "Where's your mama?"

"In her room, getting ready for the party. She's been in there all day. Opal thinks Mama's in one of her bad moods."

"On her birthday?" He set me on my feet again.

"Uh-huh. She didn't sing in the shower today. And last night she hollered at me and Opal for no reason, and then she started crying."

Daddy shook his head and took his duffel bag out of the truck. Then he reached under the seat for a bouquet of roses wrapped in wet newspaper. "Maybe these'll cheer her up."

But we both knew better. When Mama was in one of her snits, it took more than flowers to bring her around.

"Is that Mama's present?" I pointed to a box in the back of the truck.

He nodded. "But let's leave it here for now so we don't spoil the surprise." He handed me his duffel bag to carry. "Have you been practicing your fastball like I showed you?"

"Yes, sir, Daddy. Want to see?"

"As soon as we're through with supper."

We went up the steps and into the house.

"Melanie?" Daddy called out. "I'm home."

And then Mama twirled into the kitchen, smiling like the refrigerator saleslady on TV. "Hey, Duane."

"Happy birthday!" Daddy handed Mama the roses and bowed like a prince in a William Shakespeare play. "I was afraid they'd wilt before I got here. August in Texas. Hotter than the hinges of hell."

"Don't cuss," Mama said. "It's not refined."

Daddy laughed and swept her into his arms and kissed her with loud smacking sounds until she started giggling.

"Duane Hubbard, behave yourself!" she said. But she was smiling, a hopeful sign that relaxed the knot in my stomach that all week had been winding tighter and tighter.

For days Mama had been jumpy as a long-tailed cat in a roomful of rockers. She'd tried to hide it, but

Opal and I noticed how she looked right past us when we talked to her, like she was seeing something else entirely. Plus, she was in constant motion. When she crossed her legs, her foot jiggled, and her fingernails drummed on the tabletop. Late at night she prowled the kitchen, cleaning cupboards and banging pans just like she'd done the year I turned ten, when she'd left us and headed for Nashville.

For as long as I could remember, Mama had the idea that she could be the next big thing in Music City if only she could get there. Performing at the Ryman Auditorium was her one dream in life. The time she left us, she got as far as Dallas before Daddy caught up with her and sweet-talked her into coming home. Since then, me and Opal have had to stay alert for signs she might leave again. Trying to keep your mama from running off is exhausting. I was glad Daddy was home, even if only for one day.

Mama put her roses in a vase and finished setting the table. Then Opal came running down the hall and Daddy picked her up and twirled her around.

"Daddy!" she yelped. "Put me down. I just finished curling my hair and you're getting it all messed up."

"Oh, don't be a fussbudget. You'd look pretty if you were bald-headed."

Opal waved him away, but any fool could see how Daddy's compliment pleased her. She said, "The chicken is ready for the pan."

"Okay," Daddy said, "but first . . ."

Me and Opal started laughing because we knew what was coming next. A shaving cream company had put up silly advertising rhymes along the highways, and Daddy brought us a new one every time he came home.

He said, "Here's one I saw this morning. 'Spring has sprung, the grass has riz, where last year's careless driver is.'"

Then me and Opal yelled, "Burma-Shave!"

"I don't see what's so funny," Mama said. "It's downright tragic, if you ask me. And besides, there is no such word as 'riz.'"

"Oh, Mama, don't be a spoilsport," Opal said. "It's just for fun. Besides, it reminds people to drive carefully."

If there was anybody in the great state of Texas who needed good driving reminders, it was Mama. Behind the wheel she was a regular menace, driving too fast, singing too loud, stomping on the brakes half a second before the traffic lights turned from yellow to red.

Daddy tied one of Mama's aprons over his jeans and started heating oil in the iron skillet we used for frying chicken. When the oil was smoking hot, Opal dipped the chicken pieces in egg batter and flour, and dropped them into the pan. Daddy dug a fork out of the drawer and started turning the chicken as it browned, all the while telling us about the men on the *World Explorer,* and that last Thursday they had helped rescue a man who had abandoned his rig after his welding torch sparked a fire.

"You see?" Mama was sitting at the table, watching us make dinner. "I told you it's dangerous out there. You'll get yourself killed one of these days, Duane Hubbard. Then what?"

Daddy kissed her on the nose. "You worry too much. Hand me that platter."

Me and Opal set out our feast, and an hour later the four of us were sitting at the kitchen table, full as ticks. The fan turned in a slow half-circle, blowing the hot, stale air. On the TV in the living room, the news announcer talked about the Olympics coming up in Rome, Italy, the integration sit-ins happening all over the place, and whether Senator Kennedy could be elected president and save our country from the Communists.

A couple of years before, the Russians had sent some satellites called Sputniks into space and the Communists had held a big convention in New York City. Ever since, people were scared the Communists would take over America. At school we practiced ducking under our desks and throwing our arms over our heads, in case the Russians bombed us to kingdom come. Like that would save us.

One day over lemonade and sugar cookies, Mrs. Streeter told Mama the whole world had turned topsy-turvy, and that she was more afraid of the

Negroes, who had had enough of drinking from special water fountains and staying in hotels just for colored folks, than she was of the Commies. Several Negro kids had integrated a white high school up in Arkansas, and Mrs. Streeter said it was just a matter of time before colored people took over the whole country. Mama said it was a crazy time all right, and truly amazing that the outside world was totally discombobulated, but things in Mirabeau had hardly changed at all.

As we finished Mama's birthday dinner that night, I had no idea that my own personal world was about to turn upside down too.

Daddy polished off the last drumstick and took a long drink of iced tea. Opal left the table and came back with Mama's cake. I lit the candles, two pink and white 3s we'd bought at Woolworth's. We gave Mama her presents, a quilted pot holder and an African violet from me, a lipstick from Opal. FIRE AND ICE, it said on the bottom of the tube.

"Thank you, girls!" Mama beamed first at me, then at Opal. "I don't know what I'd do without my precious gems."

The sound of her voice washed over me like a rush of warm water. Happiness worked its way up from my toes and curled around my heart. Daddy leaned over the table and kissed Mama on the lips. It was such a perfect moment I felt like bawling. I wished for a camera to capture that night, to freeze it in time, but that would have been a mistake. As I found out later on, the worst pain in the world comes from remembering a happy time when you're stuck knee-deep in misery.

"Make a wish, Mama," Opal said. "Before the fan blows your candles out."

"Oh, my land, I cannot think of a single thing to wish for."

Opal rolled her eyes at me. We both knew better. Mama knew exactly what she wanted, the one thing she'd coveted since she'd first laid eyes on it back on the fourth of July.

We were standing outside Sadler's Music Store that day, our dresses limp as yesterday's handkerchiefs, our chocolate ice-cream cones melting and running down our elbows in a brown, sticky mess. Waves of heat danced on the sidewalk and seeped through the concrete so hot it burned my feet through the soles of my sandals. I stood on one foot and then the other while Mama cupped her hands to her eyes and peered into the window.

"There it is, girls," she said, her face lit up like she'd swallowed a lightbulb. "That guitar is just like Cordell Jackson's. If your daddy asks, tell him this guitar is what I want for my birthday."

Behind Mama's back, Opal heaved an exasperated sigh. All Mama talked about was how Cordell was the most talented woman in the music business. Not only did she write and record her own songs, she produced them too. Mama was determined to be the next Cordell Jackson.

Now, watching Mama cut big slabs of her devil's food birthday cake, I could barely sit still for thinking about how happy she'd be when Daddy gave her the guitar. Mama set the cake on our plates, Opal poured everybody some more tea, and we dug in. But Daddy couldn't wait to give Mama her present. He sat on the edge of his chair, his eyes snapping with his secret. After a couple of bites, he set his fork down and headed out to the truck. "Wait here," he called to Mama. "I'll be right back."

Mama licked frosting off her fork and leaned back in her chair, craning her neck. Daddy hollered, "Don't peek!"

She laughed and winked at Opal and me, so excited she could hardly stand it. She put down her fork and covered her eyes. Then Daddy came back toting a huge box topped with a red bow.

"Ta-da!" He bent down and kissed the top of Mama's head. "Happy birthday!"

Mama looked first at the box, then at him. "Duane Hubbard, what in the world?"

Daddy ripped open the box and lifted out a vacuum cleaner. "Top of the line, sugar, and looky here. A toe switch, so you don't even have to bend over to turn it on."

11

Mama stared at him like he was from Planet Krypton, then busted out bawling.

"Aw, Melanie, don't cry," Daddy said. "If I'd known how happy this would make you, I'd have got you one long before now."

Mama jumped up, ran into their room, and slammed the door.

Daddy looked like a grenade had gone off in his hand. "What did I do?"

Opal started clearing the dishes. "We told you what she wanted, Daddy. We told you twice."

"A fancy guitar, when all she knows is three chords? That don't make a lick of sense."

"Mama says the best songs ain't nothing but three chords and the truth." I ran my finger through a gob of chocolate frosting on the side of the cake, licked it off, then handed Opal the cake plate.

"Don't say 'ain't,'" Opal said. "People will think you're ignorant." She turned back to Daddy. "Women don't want practical things for their birthdays. You're supposed to give them something romantic, or something fun."

"I brought roses," Daddy said, a hurt expression in his eyes. "I think that's pretty romantic."

"Mama had her heart set on that guitar."

"Giving her that guitar would be the same as saying it's okay to run off to Nashville chasing some foolish notion that doesn't have a prayer of coming true."

Daddy rubbed his chin. "I love your mama a whole lot, but let's face it. She can't sing worth a flip. Getting turned down by those music people would break her heart."

I thought about the summer when I was nine and read *Black Beauty* for the first time, and how I dreamed of having a horse of my own. Mama said we couldn't afford one, and anyway we had no place to keep a horse. She said that holding on to a dream was almost as good as having it come true, but it didn't seem like holding on to her dream was enough for Mama.

Daddy went out to the front porch, and me and Opal washed the dishes. When we finished, we poured some more tea and took our glasses out to the back steps. It was still hot enough to fry eggs on the sidewalk. Lightning bugs flashed in Mama's Queen Elizabeth rosebushes. The last of the sunlight glittered in the trees.

I dug my toes into the silky dust, fighting the choked feeling in my throat. It was hard to take, how fast Mama's special day had gone wrong. But lately it seemed like everything was more complicated. Last year everything was easier. Opal and I spent whole days hunting arrowheads on the riverbank, making Christmas ornaments out of tinfoil, or wandering around downtown. We'd start at one end of Central Avenue, passing by the dentist's office and Mirabeau Hardware, then we'd thumb through the new magazines at the drugstore and stop in at the Purple Cow for chocolate ice cream with sprinkles. Sometimes we'd wear swimsuits under our clothes and take the long way home, down the highway and across the wooden bridge to the river where the younger kids played water tag, and the teenagers who had cars played backseat Bingo after the sun went down.

But Opal had turned fourteen in February and didn't have time for me anymore. Now all she wanted to do was talk on the phone, listen to her forty-fives, and write secrets in her diary, which she kept under lock and key. As if I didn't know what she was writing about.

I took a gulp of iced tea. Far off, lightning flashed.

"Looks like rain." Opal stretched out her legs, fished an ice cube out of her glass, and crunched it with her teeth. In the soft light, with the summer sun still glowing on her skin, my sister was the spitting image of Mama—blond and blue-eyed, so fragile-looking people fell all over themselves taking care of her. Mama said I took after Daddy's people—brown-haired, plain, and sturdy enough to take care of myself. But I didn't feel sturdy at all. Not with Mama holed up in her room crying, and Daddy sitting alone on the front porch with nothing but his hurt feelings for company.

In the morning he'd be gone again, and I was afraid for him to go away mad, afraid he might decide not to come back. I watched the clouds roll in, trying to think of some way to fix everything that had gone wrong, but I couldn't think of anything. As much as Daddy loved baseball, I didn't think watching me practice my fastball would be enough to cheer him up. And it was no use talking to Mama. When she got mad, she stayed mad for quite a while.

"Can you believe he gave her a vacuum cleaner?" Opal sighed and crunched another piece of ice. "I swear, Garnet, men are thick as fence posts. That's why I'm never getting married."

"You will if Waymon Harris asks you."

Opal shot me a look. "What do you know about it?"

"You're hoping he'll be at the howdy dance next week. Plus, you're dying to sit beside him in homeroom next year."

The mention of school made us both grin. We loved getting ready for a new year. I liked the starchy feel of new clothes, and the way my shoes hugged tight to my feet after a whole summer of going barefoot. I loved the smells of chalk and lemon floor polish, and the yeasty smell of rolls baking in the cafeteria. Most of all, I liked sitting in the dark auditorium watching films about archaeologists searching for the lost tribes of Africa, or scientists discovering the atom. Subjects that made you think you could do anything you wanted in life, even if you came from a small town like Mirabeau, Texas.

Opal lifted her hair off her neck and let it fall. "Waymon might not even be in my homeroom," she said, taking up her favorite subject again. "There's a good chance he will be, though." She pretended not to care one way or the other, but the way she mooned over Waymon's name told a different story. "Harris comes right before Hubbard, and I don't think they'd break up the *H*s. Would they?"

Before I could answer, Opal grabbed my shirt. "Wait a minute. How did you know about the howdy dance? If you've been reading my diary, Garnet Hubbard, say your prayers and prepare to die."

"If you kill me, you'll never find out."

She grabbed an ice cube from her glass and stuffed it down my shirt. I rubbed one of mine into her hair, then took off running. She caught me from behind and we rolled on the grass like TV wrestlers, until we were both weak with laughter. My sister pinned me to the ground. "Well?"

"Opal and Waymon, sitting in a tree," I panted. "K-i-s-s-i-n-g."

"You *have* been reading my stuff, you little snoop!" She let go of my arms and jumped up. "Let's go in," she said, slapping at her legs. "I'll kill you later. The mosquitoes are eating me alive."

She hauled me to my feet and peered into my face, her eyes clear as rain. "Listen. Don't tell Mama I like Waymon, okay? You know she goes crazy every time I mention boys. Just because she eloped with Daddy she acts like I'm going to run off with the first boy who asks me."

"I won't tell. And I didn't read your diary. All I have to do is listen when you're on the phone with Linda." I slapped a mosquito off my arm. "Besides, Mama's so mad she probably won't talk to us for a week."

"As if the whole vacuum cleaner mess is our fault." Opal held the screen door open for me and we went in. "Poor Daddy."

We left our glasses on the counter in the kitchen and went down the hall, past our parents' room. A sliver of light, and Mama's voice, raw with tears, spilled out.

"Nobody in this family cares what I want!" Mama was shouting. The sound of breaking glass brought me and Opal to a dead stop outside their door. I wondered what Mama had smashed to smithereens this time. Last time it was a red and yellow vase Daddy had brought her from Mexico. Later, when she got over her mad spell, Mama glued the vase back together, but it was never the same. You could see cracks running all through it.

Daddy answered Mama, his voice too low to hear. More glass broke. Then Daddy's voice rose. "You want to run off chasing some dream that's only going to break your heart. What about me? What about the girls?"

"Yes, what about the girls? I have spent every day of the past fourteen years taking care of them and I am sick of it. It's your turn!"

A roaring started deep inside my chest and rose to my ears, so I couldn't hear what Daddy said back to

her. They'd fought plenty of times, but this felt different. It felt like the end of everything. I wanted to run,
but it was like I was glued to the floor, listening to the
sounds of my family coming apart.

Then we heard Daddy's footsteps coming toward
the hallway. Opal dragged me down the hall to our
room and slammed the door. I was crying by then, my
heart stumbling on the thought that Mama didn't want
us anymore. But Opal's expression was hard and flat.

"What if she really does it this time?" I asked.
"What if she picks up and goes to Nashville and never
comes back?"

"Who cares? If she wants to go, let her go." Opal
dragged a brush through her hair. Her eyes met mine
in the mirror, and when she saw how scared I was, her
voice got softer. "Don't worry about it. Nashville's just
a dream, to get her through the hard times." She
jumped onto her bed and strummed her hairbrush
like it was a guitar. "It's o-nly make be-lie-ee-ve."

That was Mama's favorite Conway Twitty song, the
one she played over and over again. I thought of how
she made us stop talking every time it came over the
radio. I could be in the middle of asking an important
question about my homework, or trying to figure out
which dress to wear for picture day; it didn't matter.
Mama just had to hear every word of that song. It was
amazing, how she could be standing in the kitchen,
shelling peas or slicing tomatoes, and yet seem to be

somewhere else altogether. Even more amazing: I had got all the way to twelve years old before realizing Mama wished I'd never been born.

We heard the TV come on in the living room, but neither of us wanted to face Daddy right then; we didn't know what to say. The rain had started, so we stayed in our room and listened to Opal's records for a while. I tried to get a head start on my summer reading, but the problems facing Huck Finn seemed tame compared to mine, and I gave up. After the ten o'clock news, Daddy turned the TV off. Opal stripped off her shorts and T-shirt and pulled on her baby doll pj's. She tossed my faded orange Texas Longhorns nightshirt onto my bed and switched on the fan. "Okay if I read for a while?"

"I don't care."

She went into the bathroom and brushed her teeth, then flopped onto her bed and opened her copy of *A Thousand Hints for Teens*. She'd bought it by mistake, thinking it was a fan magazine, but now it was her Bible. Sometimes she read aloud from chapters like "Beauties Aren't Born, But Made" and "How to Talk to Boys." But that night she just flipped the pages back and forth, then snapped off the light.

I lay in the dark for a while, listening to the rain dancing on the roof and the quiet hum of the fan, hoping Opal was right and that everything would be normal when I woke up. The next thing I knew, it was morning and Mama was bending over me, calling my name.

I played possum. I didn't want to open my eyes and see her face for fear I'd start bawling again. But she switched off the fan and the August heat pressed down on me. Then it was either wake up or suffocate. I opened one eye. Across the room Opal was still asleep, her mouth open, one arm thrown across her forehead.

I sat up. Our room looked the same: The watercolor picture I'd painted in sixth grade and the blue ribbon I'd won for it at the county fair were still hanging on the wall next to my horse posters. Opal's portable phonograph sat in the corner, her collection of forty-fives stacked up like pancakes. Her lipstick collection and an unopened bottle of My Sin perfume she was saving to wear for You-Know-Who spilled across the dresser. But now everything felt as foreign as Timbuktu, because Mama looked at us and saw everything that was wrong with her life.

"Wake up," Mama said again, despite the fact that I was already sitting straight up, watching her. She wore a white dress with tiny red dots all over it, a red belt pulled tight at her waist, and her good summer shoes—white high-heeled pumps with gold butterflies on the toes. On her wrist was the charm bracelet Daddy had given her a long time ago, before the yelling started. She reminded me of an expensive present, all wrapped up and tied with a bow.

She shook Opal's shoulder. "Come on, baby. Rise and shine."

"Go away," my sister mumbled, but then the heat got to her, too. She sat up, shoved her hair from her eyes, looked Mama over, and said, "Who died?"

"That's not nice." Mama's voice sounded raw. "If there's anything I hate, it's a kid with a smart mouth."

"If there's anything *I* hate, it's a mother who tells lies!" I yelled. The words formed themselves, escaped my mouth before I could stop them. I expected Mama to get mad, to ask me what I meant. But she didn't say a word. Instead she pulled her truck keys from her pocket.

CHAPTER TWO

I shot Opal an I-told-you-so look. Mama was going to Nashville and never coming back.

Opal turned her ice-hard eyes on Mama. "Where's Daddy?"

But Mama wasn't ready to talk. Instead she started emptying our closet, dumping our jeans and dresses, sandals and tennies onto Opal's bed. When the closet was empty, she started in on the dresser drawers, taking out my underwear and socks, our swimsuits, and Opal's day-of-the-week panties. Finally she said, "Daddy left early to miss the traffic. He said to tell you bye, and he'll call soon."

I pictured my daddy on his ship in the middle of the Gulf of Mexico, a long way from anywhere, and tears pushed at the back of my throat. Then Mama said, "Garnet, get the suitcase."

I pulled the green suitcase from under my bed, the one we got the year Daddy drove us clear to Dallas for the Texas State Fair. Mama piled our stuff in it, everything all jumbled together, not folded neatly like she's always after us to do, and then I realized she was taking us with her. Even though I was worried sick about Daddy, my insides felt a little bit lighter. Mama couldn't have meant what she'd said the night before. Not if we were going with her.

"Are we going to Nashville, Mama?"

"Eventually. You girls will stay in Willow Flats with your aunt Julia till I'm settled in Music City. Then I'll come back for you."

"What about Daddy?" Opal crossed her arms and glared at Mama.

"That's grown-up business, Opal. I don't believe I care to discuss it. Now hurry up. I want to get on the road before it gets any hotter."

"Aren't we ever coming back here?" I asked. Suddenly Mirabeau, Texas, seemed like the best place in the world.

"Oh, for the love of Pete!" Mama spat. "You're carrying on like Mirabeau is the garden spot of the Western world. But you just wait. Once you see Nashville, you'll never want to come back here."

Opal flopped onto her bed. "I'm not going."

"Of course you are!" Mama said. "Julia will be happy to have you."

"We don't even know her!" Opal yelled. "All my friends are here. And I don't want to miss the dance. You said I could go, Mama. It's for all the incoming freshmen. I've already picked out my dress and everything."

"There'll be plenty of dances later." Mama tapped the toe of her shoe on the hardwood floor. *Click. Click. Click.* "Don't make me drag you out of that bed, Opal."

"If Opal isn't going, then neither am I!" I folded my arms the way Daddy did when he had had enough foolishness. "You said I could go shopping for school clothes with Jean Ann. You promised!"

"Sometimes promises have to wait," Mama said. "And I am not in the mood for any more back talk." She sat on the suitcase lid and snapped it shut. "Both of you, get cleaned up and get going. I want you in the truck in twenty minutes or I'll make you wish you were. Understand me?"

I saw how eager she was to drop us off like a pair of stray kittens onto some musty old relative, and something inside me died. I pushed past her, ran down the hall to the bathroom, and slid the lock into place. I turned the water on and sat in the shower, crying until my skin wrinkled and I felt hollowed out inside. There was only one explanation for how fast everything had changed: Mama had gone crazy. I was desperate for Daddy to come back and straighten her out. But he was burning up the road between Mirabeau and New Orleans, headed for the *World Explorer*. I rubbed my hair dry, wrapped myself in the towel, and went back to our room. Opal was standing at the dresser in her pj's, raking her makeup into a paper bag. I put on the denim shorts and white T-shirt Mama had left out for me and waited while Opal got ready.

We went outside. Morning sun poured through the trees. Down the street a lawn mower started up. Mama was already sitting in the pickup, a map and her bucket purse on the seat beside her. The windows were down, and Elvis was singing on the radio. Our green suitcase and Mama's two white ones were in the back, along with some taped-up cardboard boxes and a spare tire. I climbed in next to Mama. Opal crowded in beside me and slammed the door.

"Okay!" Mama said in a voice that seemed desperate for a new start. "Nashville, here I come!"

"Aren't you going to lock up the house?" Opal didn't bother to hide her contempt, but Mama didn't even notice.

"I left the key with Mrs. Streeter," Mama said. "She'll look after things till moving day." Mama ground the gears and handed me the map. "Here, Garnet. You can navigate."

The maze of red and blue lines spreading like a cobweb over the page made my stomach hurt. Map reading was not one of my talents.

"Your aunt Julia's house is right about there."
Mama stabbed with her finger at a tiny black dot somewhere in the vicinity of Oklahoma and gunned the
engine. My back pressed into the seat as the truck
roared out of the yard and onto the blacktop. I stared
at the map. Willow Flats seemed like a foreign country,
a nothing place a hundred miles from nowhere. I stole
a glance at Opal, but her face was blank; she'd gone off
by herself to someplace I couldn't follow.

We took the road that ran past my school. The
building looked August-lonely, the windows shut
tight, except for the ones in the principal's office. Mr.
Gatewood's Ford was parked in the shade of the oaks
out front. The teachers' parking lot was empty. The
swings where the little kids play stirred in the breeze.
Sunlight bounced off the school's tin roof and poured
into the cab, so bright my eyes watered.

We passed the field where Daddy taught me to pitch
a fastball and hit fly balls, and I realized I'd left behind
my collection of baseball cards and my pitcher's glove.
But there was no use asking Mama to go back for them.
She was driving like the devil was chasing her. The
truck rumbled across the wooden bridge straddling the
river, where a couple of boys were fishing with bamboo
poles. When they saw Mama barreling down on them,
they plastered themselves against the railing and waved
as we flew past. When we reached the road to Jean
Ann's house, I couldn't stay quiet any longer.

"Wait, Mama!" I yelled above the rattle of the engine. "Can't we at least stop and say good-bye?"

"Oh, sugar, there's no time. But don't you worry. As soon as I get established, we'll throw a real party for Jean Ann and all your friends. Yours, too, Opal."

"Big whoopee," Opal said. "By then they'll be living out at Sunny Acres drooling into their oatmeal."

Opal's drama club had performed at the retirement home last spring, and the sight of all those sick old people had depressed her for weeks.

"Well, it's certainly nice to know you have so much confidence in my abilities, Opal Jane."

Five minutes later we were parked in front of Sadler's Music. Mama grabbed her purse. "I'll be right back."

Opal slid down in the seat and shook her head. "She has no idea how much I hate her."

"Daddy says we aren't supposed to say we hate anybody."

"Fine. I won't say it. But that doesn't mean it isn't true."

I chewed the insides of my cheeks until I tasted blood. I wanted to hate Mama too, so it wouldn't hurt so much to let her go. But down deep I still had a soft spot in my heart for her, because of how bad she wanted her dream to come true.

A few minutes passed and then Mama came out of the store with a guitar case in one hand, her purse and a paper sack in the other. She handed the sack through

the open window. "Those are my picks and extra
strings. Don't lose them."

She set the guitar case in the back and braced it with
the suitcases, then got behind the wheel. "Is everybody
ready?"

When we just glared at her, she looked away. "Okay,"
she said under her breath. "Okay. Here we go."

She put on her white-framed sunglasses, turned up
the volume on the radio, and started her concert. She
knew every song by heart—the words, the artist, the year
it came out, its highest number on the Billboard chart.

"'Heartbreak Hotel,'" she shouted as we reached
the highway, and the last of Mirabeau, and the last of
my old life, slid away. "Elvis's first gold record.
Nineteen fifty-six." Another song blared. *At the hop, hop,
hop.* "Danny and the Juniors!" Mama informed us.
Like we cared. "Now that was a great dancin' song."

It was after one o'clock when it finally dawned on
Mama that her children hadn't eaten a bite all day. In
a dusty town off the main highway, we stopped at a grocery store for a loaf of bread, some bologna, and Moon
Pies. Mama gave Opal a handful of change and we went
to the back of the store, dropped the money in, and
slid three cold Coca-Colas out of the cooler.

There was no place to sit down to eat in the store,
so we got back in the truck. Opal made sandwiches and
passed them around. Mama hiked her skirt and drove
with the cola bottle between her knees. "If I have to

downshift, darlin', you grab this Co-Cola fast," she said to me.

For a while we were busy eating, and the only sound was the truck engine and the songs on the radio. Then the traffic slowed and we saw a detour sign. "Shoot!" Mama said. "Hold my Co-Cola, Garnet."

I grabbed the bottle and she popped the clutch and drove down a steep hill to a rutted track below. She sped past all the cars stopped on the roadway, until we came to a gravel road. There she made a hard turn that sent me crashing into Opal's shoulder.

"Ow!" Opal shoved me with her hip. "Get off me."

"I can't help it if she's driving like a maniac!"

"Hush up!" Mama said. "Look at the map, Garnet, and tell me where we are."

I unfolded the map and tried to get my bearings but it was impossible, with Mama whipping along the rough road, the truck sliding on the loose gravel, the radio blasting, and Mama asking me every ten seconds where we were. Plus, trying not to spill her Co-Cola.

Opal grabbed the map just as we flew past a road marker. She squinted at it for a minute and yelled to Mama, "We're on some farm road, about forty miles south of Mount Springs. You can get back on the highway there."

Mama nodded. "Where's my Coke?"

I handed her back the bottle and she drank it down, her eyes on the road. The radio station faded to static, and Mama worried the dial until she found another one. She kept singing and announcing the play list: Buddy Holly, Bobby Darin, Patsy Cline.

We rounded a curve and Mama hit the brakes. In front of us was a truck with a sprayer on the back, spewing fresh tar on the gravel. The stench rolled through the truck. My eyes watered. Moon Pie and bologna burned sour and hot at the back of my throat.

Mama leaned on the horn. The driver stuck his arm out the window and turned his palm up, like he was asking her what she expected him to do. The road was narrow and too curvy to pass, and we'd come too far to turn back. Mama backed off, and we inched along behind the tar truck, following it up one hill and down the other.

My stomach tingled. Cold sweat rolled down my back. "Stop, Mama!" I said. "I'm going to be sick."

"Oh, you are not. Mind over matter, Garnet. Think of something else."

But then I threw up all over my sandals, the sleeve of Opal's blouse, the map, and Mama's bucket purse. Mama pulled off the road and stopped. Opal jumped out, yelling something, but I was too sick to care. My stomach heaved and heaved. Heat shimmered on the road. Black spots danced in front of my eyes. Mama ran around the front of the truck and caught me before I fell. She said something to Opal, but her words sounded far away.

"Get your head down," Mama said. "That's right, down between your knees. Now breathe." It seemed like Mama kissed the top of my head then, but maybe I imagined it. When the world came back into focus, I saw that Opal had changed her shirt. She handed me a clean one too, and gave me the rest of her Co-Cola. Mama cleaned the map with a wadded-up tissue. "Looks like there's a town between here and Mount Springs," she said. "We'll stop there for tonight."

She rubbed my back the way she used to when I was little. Back then when I was sick, I'd lie in her bed that smelled like sunshine and lemons, eating strawberry Jell-O and chicken noodle soup, playing with books of paper dolls she'd bought at the five-and-ten. She gave me pink stuff when my stomach hurt, and cherry cough medicine when I caught a cold. Pretending to be a good mother. Pretending she cared. But now she ran her fingers through her hair, sighed deeply, and said, "How about it, Garnet? Can we go now?"

When I tried to talk, a loud burp came out instead.

"Oh, that's attractive," Opal said.

"Leave her alone." Mama wadded up our soiled shirts and tossed them into the back of the truck. She wiped off the dashboard and sprayed the cab with perfume to kill the smell. Then she noticed the gobs of black tar sticking to her good summer shoes. She shot me a hard look, toed them off, and threw them in the back too. She yanked open the door. "Well, what are you waiting for? An engraved invitation? Let's get a move on."

We got back in the cab, which still stank of bologna and puke. Mama gunned the engine and we took off again. I must have slept, because the next thing I knew, it was getting dark and Mama was pulling into the Sunset Motel. There were nine cabins, an office with peeling paint on the door, and a flashing neon sign that said VACANCY. Opal and I waited in the truck while Mama went to the office. When she came back, we hauled our stuff into number six, a room that smelled of sweat and cigarettes. There were two sagging beds with dirt-brown spreads, a table and chair, and a speckled mirror. In the bathroom the faucet dripped rusty water into a cracked sink.

"Charming place, Mama," Opal said. "Who's the innkeeper, Norman Bates?"

Opal had seen that new movie about a psycho boy who ran a motel. I wasn't allowed to go, but I heard all about it from Opal. She said Tony Perkins was so cute, it was hard to believe he could be that creepy. But he scared her so bad that for a while she was afraid to take a shower unless I stood guard outside the door.

"I am much too tired for your sarcasm, Opal," Mama said. "If you don't like the accommodations, you're free to leave." She opened her suitcase. "You can pout all you want, but I am getting cleaned up, and then I am going to that drive-in we passed for a burger and a shake. You can come along or stay here. I don't care."

When the bathroom door closed behind her, Opal threw herself onto the bed. "Wow. She is really off her rocker. Wait till Daddy finds out."

"That's what I'm counting on," I said. "As soon as we get to Aunt Julia's, we'll call him. Maybe he'll come and get us in time for your dance."

"I just hope we're not stuck with this Julia person for the rest of our lives," Opal said.

"You reckon she's as crazy as Mama?"

Opal snorted. "Nobody's as crazy as Mama."

And then, right on cue, Mama's voice came sliding out of the shower. "Crazy they call me, sure I'm crazy . . ."

Opal snickered, and that set us both off. We laughed until our sides ached, until Mama twirled out of the bathroom in a cloud of Shalimar and blue satin, her face shiny clean, her hair done up in a halo of blond curls. "If you're going with me, girls, shake a leg. I'm starving."

She unpacked her makeup case and put on fresh powder and lipstick. Opal and I took turns in the bathroom, and an hour later we pulled into the drive-in. Mama found a space near the end of the row and gave our order to the carhop. Music poured from a dozen car radios all tuned to the same station. A couple of teenagers started dancing. Halfway through the song, others joined in. Under the flashing neon lights Opal's face was the very picture of sadness. I knew she was thinking about missing the howdy dance, and I got mad at Mama all over again.

The song ended and another one began.

"Be-Bop-a-Lula!" Mama opened the truck door and grabbed my hand. "Come on, Garnet. I'll teach you to dance." In her high-heeled sandals and tight blue dress, with the light shining on her golden hair, she looked so beautiful I could barely breathe. Looking at her was like looking at a painting you could never afford to buy. Part of me wanted to fall into her arms and hold on for dear life, but another part didn't want any more memories that would make it harder to let her go.

"I don't want to."

"Fine." She let go of my hand like it was a hot coal, but she kept swaying to the music. "Opal? Want to dance with your mama?"

Opal stared. "Do I want to dance with you, after you've ruined my entire life? No, Mama, I don't believe I do."

"Oh." For a moment her face fell, then our mother smiled like she was doing a commercial for toothpaste. "Suit yourself, but it's sure a waste of a good song. Gene Vincent. Nineteen fifty-six. Boy howdy, that was a great year for music."

The carhop brought our order and we ate without talking. On the way back to the motel Mama was quiet, and I could tell she was thinking hard on something. Sure enough, as soon as we were inside number six, she sat us down and said, "Listen, girls. I know you're mad at me and you think I'm not being fair. But in this life, if you want something real bad, you've got to pay the price."

Opal crossed her arms, Daddy-style. Mama went on. "You two have your whole lives ahead of you, but look at me. Past thirty, even if most people think I don't look a day over twenty-five. If I'm ever going to make a musical career, I've got to go now, before it's too late."

She took a clipping out of her bag and passed it to us. WIN A RECORDING CONTRACT! it said in red letters. PRODUCERS LOOKING FOR NEW TALENT. IT COULD BE YOU!

"I almost threw this out with the trash," Mama said. "It was lying under a tuna fish can, but I saw it just in time. I'm telling you, girls, when fate sends you a present, you don't dare send it back unopened." She folded the clipping. "I'm going to get one of those contracts. You'll see. One day you'll thank me for getting you out of Mirabeau, Texas."

"What's wrong with Mirabeau?" Opal said. "It's a nice place. I like it there."

Mama laughed. "That's just because you've never been anywhere else. You're just like your daddy. No imagination. Believe it or not, there's a whole wide world beyond the Lone Star State, and I intend to see it all."

She thought for a minute, tapping her shiny red nails on the tabletop. "I've been thinking about a new name."

"How about Judy S. Carriot?" Opal threw herself onto the bed.

"Very funny, Opal. Be as mean as you want, but I need a stage name. Nearly everybody in Nashville has one. You know what Conway's real name is? Harold Jenkins!"

"If I was stuck with a name like Harold Jenkins, I'd change it too," Opal said.

Mama ignored her. "I can't very well go to Nashville as Melanie Hubbard."

"Why not?" I asked. "It's your name. But I guess you're throwing it away too, along with me and Opal."

"I'm not throwing you away. I am sending you to visit family! It's not that I don't want you."

"That's not what you told Daddy," Opal said.

Mama's face turned red. "I'm sorry you heard that. But that's what you get for sticking your nose where it's got no business being. Besides, I didn't mean it the way it sounded."

"How did you mean it?" Opal's voice cracked, and my own throat felt tight.

Mama's eyes filled up, and for a minute I felt sorry for her, but then I thought about having to leave my whole life behind, and how she was running away from Daddy, and my insides went hard.

"There's no sense in talking more about it," Mama said. "It's plain to see you're both determined to be mad at me."

Opal dug her pajamas out of our suitcase. "I'm going to bed."

"Me too," I said. "My stomach feels funny again."

I got ready for bed and climbed under the covers. Opal slid in and turned her face to the wall. After Mama switched off the lamp, I lay wide-eyed in the dark, bone tired and achy, but too keyed up to sleep. I kept wishing I was back home in my own bed. And I couldn't stop thinking about Daddy, wondering if he'd called home yet. I turned over and punched the musty-smelling pillow, trying to sort out all the feelings churning inside me, flipping like a coin from one side to the other.

Mama was brave for going after her dream; she was the world's biggest coward for leaving Daddy and sending us away. One thing I knew for sure: A longing for the extraordinary had grabbed ahold of her and was burning her up inside, so hot and fierce that her heart had gone stone cold toward everything and everybody standing in her way. That was Mama.

Fire and ice.

CHAPTER THREE

The next afternoon, one detour, two wrong turns, and one flat tire later, we passed the signs for a bunch of Texas towns named for other places—Reno, Bogota, Paris—and then we crossed the Red River into Oklahoma. We drove north through towns so small they didn't even have stoplights, and then we left the main highway and took a blacktop road that seemed to go for a million miles before it became a washboard barely wide enough for two cars to pass.

"Almost there!" Mama said, with such a happy look on her face you'd have thought she was announcing our arrival into New York City. Trust me, Willow Flats was about as far from New York as a person could possibly get.

For as far as I could see, there was nothing but hard

brown land under a pale sky. A sluggish river shaded by willow trees ran by the side of the road. We passed a water tower that said WELCOME TO WILLOW FLATS. HOME OF THE 1948 STATE CHAMPION WARRIORS. On down the road was a redbrick high school with a gym at one end and a gravel driveway at the other.

"That's where I went to junior high and high school," Mama said, laughing, "when I had nothing more exciting to do. Graduated dead last in my class. Julia was first in hers. People always said I got the beauty and she got the brains."

"All the kids go to school in the same building?" Opal asked.

Mama stopped the truck on the side of the road, as if her school was a world-famous tourist attraction we didn't dare miss. "Everybody from seventh grade through seniors. When Julia was a girl, even the elementary school kids went there. But they finally got a school of their own."

Then I saw that across the road from the high school was a smaller school made of the same red brick. Behind a chain-link fence was a weedy playground with a couple of seesaws and some swings.

"Can we go now?" Opal shifted in the seat. "I feel like a sardine squished into a can."

Mama ground the gears and we took off again. Through the windshield I saw tin-roofed houses and miles of pastures dotted with faded barns and falling-down chicken coops. In one yard an old car with no tires sat atop concrete blocks. We passed a feed store, a stinking cattle yard, a Texaco gas station, and three Baptist churches.

I decided Aunt Julia wasn't nearly as smart as Mama gave her credit for. How else could you explain why she'd spent her whole life in a place like Willow Flats?

"What a dump," Opal muttered.

It was true. Nothing looked like it did back in the piney woods of Texas. Not the road, nor the pastures, nor the buildings. Even the sky looked different, harsh and washed out.

A flatbed truck pulled out in front of us. Mama leaned on the horn, but the man behind the wheel was in no hurry. Since we couldn't pass him without breaking an axle, we slowed to a crawl and followed him past a hardware store and a bait shop advertising live worms. We passed the courthouse, a squatty-looking building with a clock tower and an arched doorway. On a bench out front sat the world's oldest living human being. His skin was the color of an old baseball mitt, and his long gray hair fell to his waist. He wore a beat-up ten-gallon hat, a pair of jeans, and a pair of black high-tops. As we inched past, his eyes followed us for a moment. Then he went back to his whittling.

"Well, I'll be!" Mama said. "That's Charlie Twelve-trees. I thought for sure he'd have passed on by now."

"What kind of a name is Twelvetrees?" Charlie was

the first interesting thing I'd seen since we arrived, and I twisted around in my seat for another look.

"Cherokee, I think," Mama said.

The flatbed driver turned onto a dirt road and honked at us. Mama gunned the engine and the truck jerked and bucked on the rutted road. Hot wind poured through the cab. Mama went on. "When I was a girl, Charlie lived in the caretaker's cottage at the old Higby mansion out on the highway. It was a museum in those days, and he had a little shop where he sold his carvings to tourists." She laughed. "He used to tell them the carvings were magic. Imagine!"

We passed an orchard and a rusty mailbox with its lid hanging open. Mama pulled off the main road and onto a dirt lane that led to a run-down house half-hidden behind a row of lilac bushes. We had come to the edge of the livable world. "Well, girls," Mama announced, tapping the horn, "we're here."

The front door opened, and out came Aunt Julia. She wore a pair of thick-soled boots minus their laces, a faded denim dress, and an apron trimmed with yellow rickrack. She was carrying a sharp knife. Not the most promising of beginnings.

"Melanie!" she cried.

Mama got out of the pickup and said, "Hey there, Julia. How are you?"

"Alive and kicking." Aunt Julia stuck her head into the open window of the truck and gave us the once-over. "So," she said. "The precious gems. The only other time I saw you two, weren't neither one of you bigger than a minute."

"And whose fault is that?" Mama rounded the truck and gave our aunt an awkward pat on the shoulder. She tried to keep her voice light, but I could tell from the way she fiddled with her hair that she was nervous. "I've begged you for years to visit."

"Last time I looked, the roads go both ways." Aunt Julia smiled, but her eyes were wary. Watching her and Mama was like watching two boxers circling the ring before the first punch.

Me and Opal got out of the truck. I finger-combed my hair and smoothed the wrinkles in my shirt, trying to make a good impression. Opal crossed her arms and ankles and leaned against the fender. Aunt Julia said, "Opal is her mama made over, but you, Miss Garnet, are the spittin' image of your daddy. How's he doing, anyhow?"

"Same as always," Mama put in quickly. "Working too much. You know how men are."

Aunt Julia nodded like she knew exactly what Mama meant, though as far as I knew, our aunt had never been married.

Mama took our suitcase out of the truck.

"I'll take that," Aunt Julia said. She folded her knife and dropped it into her apron pocket. "Go on in. I've made supper."

"I can't stay," Mama said. "I need to get to Nashville. I've got about a billion things to do. Find a place to stay, do some laundry, *and*"—she paused for dramatic effect—"find a place to cut my demo record. I swear, I get so excited just thinking about it, I nearly pee in my pants."

"Melanie!"

"Well, I do! Just think, Julia, this time next year, I'll be singing at the Ryman like Cordell Jackson. And you'll be there in the front row. You and my two precious gems. You'll see."

"What about Daddy?" Opal asked, narrowing her eyes.

Mama looked away. "Well, of course, Daddy, too. If he wants to come." She threw Aunt Julia one of her Hollywood smiles. "Opal's fourteen. There's no pleasing her."

Then Mama grabbed Opal and me and hugged us hard. "Be good, and mind your aunt Julia. I'll be back to get you as soon as I'm settled."

"Before school starts?" I asked. If I was going to have to go to a new school up in Nashville, I wanted to be there from Day One. It's no use trying to make friends once everybody has staked out their territory.

"I'll try. Just wait till you see the stores in Nashville. We'll have ourselves a big time, shopping for new stuff." She turned to my sister. "Opal? You look after Garnet. And don't give Aunt Julia a hard time. Just remember, you're family, not guests. I expect you to help out around here."

Aunt Julia shaded her eyes with one hand. "Drive carefully, Melanie. And keep your doors locked. It'll be dark soon and the world is full of crazy people."

"Amen," Opal muttered.

If Mama heard that, she didn't let on. She climbed into the truck, took an oversize envelope out of the glove compartment, and handed it to Aunt Julia. Then she cranked the engine and made a U-turn in the yard. "You watch the mailbox, honey," she said to me. "I'll send you a real nice surprise. Bye-bye now!"

Aunt Julia stood between Opal and me, our suitcase at her feet, Mama's envelope tucked under her arm. "Wave bye to your mama, girls."

I couldn't do it. I was too stunned at how fast my whole life had turned into something I could barely recognize, and it hurt too much to see Mama's truck getting smaller and smaller until it was lost in a cloud of Oklahoma dust. I felt like Mama had dumped me on the moon and said, "There you go. Figure out how to survive." I tried not to cry, but hot tears spilled down my face.

"Don't you dare start bawling," Opal said, her voice tight. "She's not worth it."

"Don't bad-mouth your mama, Opal Jane," Aunt Julia said. "She has her faults, but she's the only mama you've got. Come on. Let's go in."

We went up the porch steps. A gray cat sauntered out from under the porch swing and wrapped itself around Aunt Julia's leg.

"Get off me, Mozart," she scolded. "I'm busy."

I reached down to pet him, but he hissed and arched his back like I'd gone after him with a pickax, and my tears came back. Even the stupid cat didn't want me.

"He's not used to strangers," Aunt Julia said. "Go on in. I reckon you're hungry."

We went inside. Mozart shot past my legs and hid in the kitchen. Aunt Julia left our suitcase by the stairs and showed us to the table. It was set for four, with white dishes and glasses with yellow flowers etched on them. On shelves above the old-fashioned sink were jars of strawberry preserves, green beans, and purple beets. Cookbooks, a toaster, and a clock shaped like a rooster sat on the counter.

"Sit down, you two," our aunt said.

I was anxious to call Daddy, but I folded my hands in my lap and tried not to look at the empty chair where Mama belonged. Aunt Julia switched on a light and clomped around in her heavy shoes getting napkins and filling our glasses with ice. Then she dished up enough food to feed the Confederate army: peas, tomatoes, fried okra, a roasted chicken, watermelon, and iced tea with lemon slices floating in it. It was the finest meal I'd seen since Mama's birthday, and I told Aunt Julia so.

"Don't expect it every day," she said.

"No, ma'am, I won't."

Aunt Julia picked up her fork. I kept my eyes on my plate. She said, "Well, what are you waiting for? Dig in."

We ate without saying much. After we finished, Opal and I helped with the dishes, and then Aunt Julia gave us a tour of the house. The living room was full of old-fashioned furniture, heavy and dark. There was a sofa with oak leaves carved into its wooden back, a floor lamp with gold tassels hanging off the shade, a piano, and an ancient radio in a wooden cabinet the size of a refrigerator.

"No TV?" I whispered to Opal.

Aunt Julia continued the tour down a dark hall that led to her room, a bathroom, and a back porch that faced the orchard.

"Aunt Julia?" Opal said. "We need to call our daddy. He doesn't know where we are."

"He knows. Your mama called him before she called Sunday Larson's store to tell me she was on her way here with you."

"Do you work at Larson's?"

"No, Larson's is the nearest phone, that's all."

My sister went white as a slice of bread. "You don't have a phone?"

"Don't need one."

Aunt Julia picked up our suitcase and motioned

us up the stairs. "I've made up Melanie's old room for you."

We went up the creaking stairs to a room with twin beds, a white painted dresser with an oval mirror, and a narrow closet squashed under the eaves. Two windows looked out to the apple orchard and a garden where dozens of pink and purple whirligigs twirled in the breeze.

Aunt Julia saw me studying them and said, "I made those myself. Carving whirligigs is my hobby."

Which explained why she'd met us at the door with a knife in her hand. I thought of Charlie Twelvetrees and his magic carvings. It seemed like whittling was the major pastime in Willow Flats, Oklahoma.

"Bathroom's down the hall on your left," Aunt Julia said. "Don't use up all the hot water, and don't leave your wet towels on the floor. I'm not running a hotel."

"Right," Opal muttered. "In a hotel they have to be nice to you."

"What was that, Opal?" Aunt Julia said.

"Nothing, Aunt Julia. Good night."

It was barely dark outside, but after two scorching days in the truck with Mama, I was dead tired. I brushed my teeth, splashed some water on my face, changed into my Longhorns nightshirt, and fell onto the bed. June bugs batted against the window screen. The smell of cut grass drifted on the breeze, reminding me of home. I thought of how happy Daddy had looked the night of Mama's party, so excited to give her the vacuum cleaner, and his bewilderment when everything fell apart. I tried to cry without making noise, but Opal heard me anyway.

"Garnet? Are you okay?"

"I miss Daddy. I want to go home."

"Me too." Opal sighed. "The dance is next Saturday. I'll bet Linda already has a date. And I'm stranded out here in the sticks."

I wiped my eyes and counted on my fingers. "If Daddy left tomorrow, he could be here by Tuesday. We could still make it home in time."

"We have to find a phone! I'll die if Waymon shows up at the dance and I'm not there." Opal was quiet for a moment. The cicadas sang in the silence.

"Aunt Julia hates us," I said.

"I think she's just upset because Mama dumped us here with hardly any warning," Opal said. "But guess what? I don't care if she *does* hate us. I didn't ask to come here." She dug through the suitcase for her baby doll pj's. "What's with her shoes? They look like combat boots."

"Maybe that's the style up here."

"It wouldn't surprise me." Opal pulled on her pj's and got into bed. "Get some sleep, if you can."

I closed my eyes and tried to sleep, but everything felt all wrong. I wanted to be back in my own room, in my own bed that squeaked when I turned a certain way.

I wanted the hum of traffic going past our house on Piney Road, and the voice of the TV newsman coming through the wall. And Mama in the kitchen, singing along with Elvis and Conway.

Here in Oklahoma there was nothing but the sighs of the old house settling down for the night, the memory of Aunt Julia's grim face, and the musty smell of an unused room. I could tell Opal was still awake, and it felt like we were the only two people in the world. I wondered if Mama was awake too. I imagined her driving along a dark, lonesome highway. Behind my closed eyelids was a map of red and blue lines taking her farther and farther away.

"I wonder where Mama is by now," I said.

"Who cares?" Opal flopped onto her stomach. "Go to sleep, will you? I'm beat."

I must have finally slept, because the next thing I knew, Aunt Julia was standing in the room, pulling back the curtains, letting in the sun.

"Wake up, you two! It's Sunday morning, and going on ten o'clock. The Lord will be expecting to hear from us."

I stifled a groan. I could think of thirty-seven ways to spend a summer Sunday, and not one of them involved sitting on a hard bench listening to somebody yell at me for all the ways I had disappointed the Almighty since last week.

In her bed Opal stirred. "Is it morning already?"

"Morning's nearly gone," Aunt Julia said. "There's time for cornflakes if you hurry." She glanced at her watch. "You've got half an hour. It's a long walk to the church."

Opal squinted at our aunt. "Did you say 'walk'?"

"I did indeed."

"Where's your car?"

"Don't have one."

"Great," Opal said. "That's just peachy."

She stood up real slow and swayed for a minute, like an actress in a death scene. "Oooh. All of a sudden I feel woozy. Maybe I'd better not go."

"Nice try, Miss Barrymore," our aunt said, "but no cigar."

"That's all right," Opal shot back. "I don't smoke."

Aunt Julia pulled my pink skirt and white blouse and Opal's blue dress out of the suitcase. "These will do. I'll meet you in the kitchen."

She draped our clothes over the end of my bed. "Hurry up. I don't want to be late."

When the door closed behind her, Opal fell onto her bed. "How much worse can our lives get? No TV, no car, and no phone. We might as well be in jail. I swear, when Mama comes back, I'm going to wring her neck for this." She got up and grabbed a pair of panties out of the suitcase. "The sooner we call Daddy the better. I'll shower first."

"Okay. Hey, Opal? Today's Sunday."

"So?"

"You've got your Tuesday panties."

"Ask me if I care."

We were so anxious to call Daddy that we broke our all-time speed record for getting ready. Half an hour later we were dressed, fed, and heading down the road with Aunt Julia. Opal marched ahead, her sandals kicking up little clouds of dust. Aunt Julia talked about tomatoes and her whirligigs and the new preacher. By the time we could see the church up ahead, a plain white building sitting in a patch of dead grass, we had learned all about Reverend Underwood and his red-headed wife, Arlene; their daughters, Faith and Hope; and their half-blind cocker spaniel, Smitty. We knew the rev drove a Buick and that he had gone to preacher school in Fort Worth, Texas.

At the church door an old man in a shiny blue suit handed us a program. We went in and sat in the back row. "It's cooler back here," Aunt Julia said, settling into the pew.

Huge, throbbing blisters had formed on both my heels. I slid my feet out of my sandals and looked around. Down front was Arlene the carrot-top, and two shorter redheads I figured must be the daughters. The taller of the two turned around like she had eyes in the back of her head and had caught me staring at her. She glanced at me like I was yesterday's newspaper and whispered into her mother's ear.

Then a woman wearing a white dress and the world's tallest beehive hairdo slid onto the piano bench, flipped through her sheet music, and began to play. The pews filled up. A baby wailed. Pretty soon after that the door opened and Mr. Underwood came in.

He lifted his arms. We stood and sang. Prayed and sat. Heat pressed onto me like a heavy curtain. Sweat trickled down my back. I stole a glance at my sister. Opal was busy peeling off her nail polish; hot-pink flakes of it curled and fell onto her lap. I picked up a cardboard fan off the pew and handed it to her. Aunt Julia got out her glasses and opened her Bible.

Mr. Underwood cleared his throat and I braced myself for the usual warnings about sin, and how if people didn't shape up, they would not go to be with Jesus when they died but would instead spend eternity in h-e-double-l. But he shuffled a stack of newspaper clippings and began to read.

"It says here, in the *Daily Oklahoman,* that Negro children were enrolled for the first time last week at a white public school in Virginia." He held the clipping between his fingers and let it fall. It drifted down and landed on the carpet right in front of the three redheads.

"And we've got that young senator from Massachusetts who wants to be the first Catholic president of the United States of America. They say if he's elected, he's planning to send a man to the moon and back."

A whole handful of clippings rained onto the carpet like birthday party confetti. "Think of that," the preacher said. "A man on the moon, when it hasn't been but fifty-odd years since the Wright brothers invented the airplane."

I fanned my face. The backs of my legs were stuck to the pew. You'd think the preacher would have made short work of his sermon, seeing how miserable we were, but he was just getting started.

"It's scary when change rains down on us faster than we can comprehend it," he said. "Who can know what tomorrow will bring?"

As desperate as I was to get out of there, I found myself agreeing with him. Just Thursday night we'd had a birthday party for Mama. And look at what all had changed since then.

He went on talking. I tried to pay attention, but my thoughts kept circling back to Mama and what she'd done, and to Daddy, drifting around sad and alone somewhere in the Gulf of Mexico. I wanted to believe that Mr. Underwood was right, and God was in charge of everything, but it felt as if God had been called somewhere else on a big emergency and left the Hubbard family on its own.

Finally the preacher ran out of steam. We sang "Rock of Ages" and the service was over. I shoved my feet into my sandals, peeled myself off the pew, and followed Opal and Aunt Julia into the sunlight.

Aunt Julia mopped her face and checked her watch. "Pot roast'll be done by the time we get home. Are you girls hungry?"

"A little," I said. "But could we call my daddy first?"

"I don't see what good it will do, but all right." She dropped her handkerchief into her purse and snapped it shut. "Larson's is closed on Sunday, but you can use the phone at the Texaco station if you don't mind walking some more."

Pain shot through my blistered feet, but I wanted to talk to Daddy so bad I didn't care if they rotted off. "I don't mind."

Just then the preacher came out of the crowd and shook Aunt Julia's hand.

Aunt Julia introduced Opal and me. "The girls are visiting for a while."

He smiled down at us. "Welcome to Willow Flats. My daughters are here somewhere. They're about your age. Maybe you'd like to come to our young people's hayride on Saturday night. We'll take the wagon out to the Cooleys' farm for hymn singing, and come back here for peach ice cream."

"Thanks," Opal said. "But we won't be staying that long."

"I'm sorry to hear that. Our church needs more

young people. If your plans change, just come on over. We'll leave here around six thirty."

Aunt Julia said, "If we're going to the Texaco, we should get started. I don't want my roast to burn."

Mr. Underwood said, "Pardon me, Miss Julia. You're walking all that way?"

"It's important," I said.

"I'm used to it," Aunt Julia said.

"But in this heat?" The preacher waved to his wife, who was standing with a group of women in the yard. He pointed to us and made a driving motion with his hands. She nodded and went back to her conversation. "Come with me. I'll drive you to the station and then take you home."

"We don't want to be any bother," Aunt Julia said.

But then Opal turned her baby blues on the preacher, smiled sweetly, and said, "Thank you so, so much, Reverend. We'd really appreciate it."

We followed him across the parking lot, past rows of pickup trucks and dusty sedans plastered with Nixon decals and Kennedy bumper stickers, and climbed into the Preachermobile.

"That's odd," Aunt Julia said when we got to the Texaco to find it empty. "It's not like Harold to run off and leave everything unattended. Anyway, the phone's back here, girls. Now, don't talk but a minute or two. Long distance is expensive."

She and the preacher went back outside and stood

in the shade. Mr. Underwood took off his jacket and rolled up his sleeves. He bought a grape Nehi from the cooler and drank it while Aunt Julia talked.

Opal dialed the number of the office in Louisiana that would switch us through to Daddy's ship-to-shore radio. "It's ringing!" she said at last. I stood next to her with my ear pressed hard to the receiver. I couldn't wait to talk to Daddy, to say something that would make up for Mama's bad behavior, and to beg him to come and take us back to civilization.

The phone rang and rang.

"Maybe you dialed the wrong number," I said.

"No, I didn't."

We waited through ten more rings before Opal hung up.

"We'll try again tomorrow," I said. "We'll call every day if we have to."

Aunt Julia came in. "That was quick."

"We didn't get through," Opal said.

"It's just as well," Aunt Julia said. "Come on, let's not keep the reverend waiting."

On the way to Aunt Julia's, the preacher talked about the Sunday school lessons he was writing and about the choir his wife was organizing. "Arlene can't wait to get started," he said. "How about it, Miss Julia? You've got a fine voice, and altos are in short supply."

Aunt Julia stared out the window and fiddled with

the clasp on her purse. "My sister is the singer in the family."

Just as we reached the turnoff to Aunt Julia's, a rusted-out truck came tearing along the road toward us. The preacher slowed as it rattled past.

"That looked like Harold's truck," Aunt Julia said, turning around in her seat. "I wonder what he's doing way out here."

Mr. Underwood swung the car into the lane and cut the engine. Aunt Julia opened the car door. "Thank you, Reverend. Won't you bring your family here for dinner? There's plenty of food."

"That sounds mighty fine, but I'm already late for a meeting."

"Another time, then."

The preacher drove off. As we started up the steps, I saw a piece of notebook paper taped to the front door. For a wild moment I thought it was a note from Mama. I imagined she'd changed her mind and decided that me and Opal and Daddy were more important than some crazy dream after all. I imagined she'd gone out looking for us. "If I don't find you down at the church, I'll come back here," the note would say. "Wait for me, my precious gems. I've come to take you home."

If only that had happened, instead of what actually did.

Chapter Four

Aunt Julia sat down on the porch swing and unfolded the note. I watched her face go pale as milk, and fear went through me like an arrow. I imagined Mama sick with a fever, or dead in a horrible crash like the Burma Shave victim. But the note had nothing to do with her.

"You girls don't deserve this," Aunt Julia said wearily, "but here it is anyhow. Your daddy's been hurt. We're supposed to call a Mr. Hancock in New Orleans."

Opal grabbed the note. "Is it bad? What happened? Where's Daddy?"

"It doesn't say." Aunt Julia rose, and the swing creaked. "Garnet, run down to the orchard. Past the whirligigs and the water pump you'll see a bat and a kettle hanging from a tree. Bang on that kettle for all you're worth, and pray Charlie Twelvetrees is at home."

I took off through the orchard to send Aunt Julia's distress signal, my feet pounding on the path, fear pushing against my skin, trying to get out. I found the bat and pounded the kettle until it bonged like a church bell. I hit and hit it until my arms quivered and my shirt was wet with sweat and tears.

Then Aunt Julia yelled for me to hurry back. Far down the road a cloud of dust boiled up. I reached the house just as a maroon Studebaker pulled into the yard, Charlie Twelvetrees at the wheel.

"Miss Julia, what's the trouble?" He reached across the seat to open the door. Opal and I scrambled into the backseat. Aunt Julia told Charlie about the note, and that we had to get to a telephone right away. She introduced me and Opal but didn't mention that our mama was AWOL.

"I'm sorry our first meeting is under such unhappy circumstances," Charlie said, his expression grave.

He spun the wheel and we headed back to town, the car floating along the road like a clumsy barge. I watched Charlie's hair blowing in the wind coming through the open car window, thinking that he sure didn't talk like the Indians on the TV. He talked like a teacher, or a newsman on the radio. His voice was calm and full of music, like water tumbling over rocks.

When we got to the Texaco, Opal wrenched open the car door and we scrambled out. Charlie said, "Take your time. I'll wait here."

We went into the gas station, and Aunt Julia introduced me and Opal to Harold. He shook our hands like we were grown-ups. "I sure am sorry about your daddy. But I hear they've got real good hospitals in New Orleans. They'll patch him up good as new."

He took a couple of Coca-Colas from the cooler, opened them, and passed them to us. We followed Aunt Julia to the telephone. She dialed, waited, and asked for Mr. Hancock. I stood as close to the receiver as I could, but I couldn't hear anything except Aunt Julia's side of the conversation, which was mostly "I see" and "All right." She scribbled the name of a hospital and a couple of phone numbers on the back of the note, nodded her head like the man on the other end could see her, then said good-bye and hung up.

"Why'd you hang up?" I cried. "I wanted to talk to Daddy."

"He can't talk now," Aunt Julia said. "There was a fire on the ship and he's badly burned. But he's in a good hospital, getting the best of care."

Too scared to cry, I said, "I want to see him."

"That won't be possible for a while. He's in a special room until the risk of infection is past. Mr. Hancock says we'll know more in twenty-four hours."

Opal slammed her bottle on the table so hard that Coca-Cola sloshed onto a pile of gas receipts and order forms lying on the counter. "It's Mama's fault."

"Now, Opal, you know that isn't true," Aunt Julia said.

"Yes, it is! If she hadn't run off, Daddy wouldn't have been worrying, and he would have been paying attention when the fire started. Now we don't know where the heck she is, Daddy's practically dead, and we're stuck in this stupid hick town with—"

"That's enough, Opal," Aunt Julia warned. "You girls have got a tough row to hoe, all right. But you may as well get over the notion that life is fair and the things that happen make sense."

She turned to me. "Go tell Charlie Twelvetrees I'll be there in a minute."

But I stood there like I'd turned to ice. The thought of having to shoulder one more sorrow made me too tired to move.

"Go on." Aunt Julia gave me a gentle push toward the front of the station, where Harold sat eavesdropping while pretending to read a Superman comic book. "You too, Opal."

She took the key to the ladies' room off the hook by the door. Me and Opal left our Coke bottles on the counter next to the fan belts and motor oil cans, and went out to the car. Charlie had opened all the doors to let the breeze through and was sitting sideways in the driver's seat, carving a bird from a piece of shiny black wood. I could see the bird's head, its tiny beak, and the beginning of a wing.

"What happened?" he asked, without looking up.

"A fire on my daddy's ship," I said. "He's burned, and we can't see him until he's better."

Charlie stopped whittling and looked up at me. "I'm sorry."

Opal stalked off and stood in the sliver of shade beneath the red and white Texaco awning. Charlie went back to his whittling. I watched his hands turning the wood and the curly shavings falling onto his high-tops. He had such a calm way about him, I felt like I could tell him everything, even though we'd just met.

"I'm afraid he'll die." My words came out in a dry whisper.

A long silence followed, during which Charlie's knife flashed in the light and the bird's wings, ready for takeoff, emerged from the wood. Then he said, "Death is a part of life, and not to be feared. Some say it's life's last great adventure. But I don't think it's your father's time yet."

"How do you know?"

He looked at me in a way that made me ashamed for asking, and instead of giving me a simple answer, told a story about an Apache warrior who survived a brutal battle, a raging blizzard, and a gunshot wound, any one of which could have spelled the end for him,

but the Great Spirit protected him because his purpose on Earth wasn't finished yet. It was such a good
story that for a moment I nearly forgot my worries.
Charlie handed me the finished carving, still warm
from his touch. "Keep it."

Aunt Julia came outside and we started home. I sat
in the backseat beside Opal, the little bird resting in
my palm. I was way too old to believe in magic, but that
fact didn't keep me from wishing that the Great Spirit
would watch over Daddy, and that somehow the carving held special powers that could put our torn-apart
family back together.

"Aunt Julia?"

She turned in the seat to look at me.

"We can't just sit here and wait until Mama takes a
notion to send us a postcard. Somebody has to find
her and tell her about Daddy."

"As if she cares," Opal muttered.

Aunt Julia mopped her face with a wadded-up tissue. "I don't know what to do, short of calling the
highway patrol."

"That's exactly what you should do," Charlie said.
"Give them her license plate number and they'll be on
the lookout for her."

"Do either of you know the tag number on your
mama's truck?" Aunt Julia asked.

"I don't," I said.

Opal shook her head.

Charlie pulled into the yard. "I could call the state license bureau. They can look it up."

"Thank you," Aunt Julia said in a wobbly voice. "I wish we'd thought of this before we left the station. Now you'll have to make another trip."

"The bureau is closed today," Charlie said. "But I'll be in town tomorrow to pick up feed for my chickens. It's no trouble."

He dug around in the side pocket of the car door and handed Aunt Julia a scrap of paper and the nub of a pencil. "Write down a description of the truck, and I'll see what I can do."

"The license is probably in Daddy's name," Opal said, leaning forward in her seat. "He's the one who took care of everything. That truck wouldn't even have a license plate if it was left up to Mama."

Aunt Julia wrote down all the information. Charlie stuffed the paper in his pocket. We got out of the car.

"Much obliged for the lift," Aunt Julia told Charlie.

He raised his hand in a funny salute, turned the car around, and drove away.

In the kitchen black smoke was pouring out of the oven, curling onto the ceiling.

"My roast!" Aunt Julia opened the oven door, grabbed a box of baking soda from the cupboard, and sprinkled it over the flames. The fire died, but it was too late. The roast, and the potatoes and carrots, too, were burned to a crisp.

Aunt Julia stumbled to a chair, laid her head on the table, and sobbed. I truly hated my mother then for all the misery she'd caused. She'd said there was a price to be paid for dreams, but it seemed like everyone but her was paying it. Opal and I were stuck in Willow Flats, Aunt Julia was at the end of her rope, and Daddy was clinging to life hundreds of miles away, all because Mama was convinced Nashville was her destiny. I imagined her driving barefoot along some winding road, the radio blaring, a cold Co-Cola tucked between her knees, tickled to pieces to be rid of us all and on her way to a brand-new life. But her destiny would just have to wait, I thought. Once the highway patrol found her, she'd have to turn around and come back for Opal and me. Then we'd go home and take care of Daddy.

Opal got a pair of pot holders out of the drawer and lifted the burned roasting pan onto the counter. I held the garbage pail while she scraped the burned meat and vegetables into it. Then Opal squirted some dishwashing liquid into the pan, ran some hot water into it, and left it to soak. Aunt Julia got over her crying spell, and we made lemonade and grilled cheese sandwiches and ate lunch on the porch.

Afterward Aunt Julia went in to take a nap. Opal went upstairs to get her magazine. I sat in the porch swing and held on to the magic bird so tightly his beak pricked my palm. "Okay," I told him. "Do your stuff. Make my daddy well. And bring Mama back."

CHAPTER FIVE

Monday morning the highway patrol tracked down Mama's truck at a motel on the Tennessee border and told her an emergency was brewing back in Oklahoma. But she kept going until she got to Nashville, then sent Aunt Julia a telegram. There was no phone in her room at the hotel for ladies where she was staying until her recording contract came through, but there was one at the end of the hall and she promised to call us at two o'clock the next day at Sunday Larson's store.

Opal pretended she couldn't care less what Mama had to say, but I couldn't wait to talk to her. I was sure once Mama heard what had happened to Daddy and how miserable me and Opal were in the shack at the end of the world, she'd come to her senses.

After lunch I helped Aunt Julia wash the dishes. Opal was lying on the couch with a damp towel on her forehead, nursing a headache and flipping through *A Thousand Hints for Teens*. I wished for some hints on how to make a runaway mother come back.

"Garnet," Aunt Julia said. "It's almost time to head for Sunday's place. Run out to the shed and fetch my wagon."

Opal came off the sofa like a shot. "I am *not* going to be seen in public riding in a wagon."

"Don't worry. You wouldn't fit."

"Huh?"

"It's a Radio Flyer. I use it for hauling groceries and such."

Opal groaned. "We'll look like people out of *The Grapes of Wrath*. What if somebody sees us?"

"There's no shame in being poor, Opal," Aunt Julia said. "But I won't force you to go. Your mama will be disappointed, though."

"Good!" Opal yelled. "I hope she *is* disappointed. I hope she's sick with despair at not getting to talk to her precious gem!" She grabbed her magazine off the couch. "But I wouldn't count on it. The only one Mama cares about is herself."

She pounded up the stairs and slammed the door so hard it scared the cat.

"My, my," Aunt Julia said with a long sigh. "Well, she *is* fourteen."

Like that explained everything. I went out to the shed and pulled the wagon around to the front porch. I wasn't thrilled with the idea myself, but my need to talk to Mama outweighed my embarrassment. So what if somebody from Willow Flats saw me hauling sacks of cornmeal and cans of evaporated milk in a red wagon? So what if my sourpuss aunt wore clodhoppers and clothes that went out of style when Truman was president? By the time September rolled around, I'd be long gone from Willow Flats.

Aunt Julia jammed her straw hat on her head and hollered up the stairs, "Opal? We're going now."

Me and Aunt Julia started up the road, the wagon bouncing along behind us. Aunt Julia didn't seem inclined to talk, so I concentrated on what I wanted to say to Mama. I had to plan it just right. If I acted too excited that Daddy's accident was bringing her home, she'd be mad. If I acted like I wasn't worried about him, she might decide it was okay to leave me and Opal right where we were. If I said everything was going just fine with Aunt Julia, Mama would think I didn't need her, and her feelings would be hurt, even though *she* was the one who left *me*. It was a lot to think about, and I started feeling panicky in my chest, feeling that whatever I said would be the wrong thing.

Aunt Julia stopped beneath a scraggly tree, took off her hat, and fanned herself. "Whew! It's a scorcher today."

"My feet are burning," I said. "How much farther?"

She pointed. "Just past that bend in the road is Crowly's Bait Shop, and next to that is Sunday Larson's. It won't be long now."

When we got to the store, Aunt Julia left the wagon on the porch and we went in. A frizzy-haired woman wearing faded overalls, a white shirt, and a pair of high-top basketball shoes just like Charlie's came out from behind the counter to meet us.

"Julia, are you all right?" she asked. "Harold said somebody had an accident."

"My brother-in-law, Duane," Aunt Julia said. "This is his younger daughter, Garnet."

The woman shook my hand. "Sunday Larson. Glad to meetcha! Sorry about your daddy, though." She turned back to my aunt. "What happened, Julia? Is he hurt bad? Where is he? Have you heard from Melanie? Is she in Nashville already?"

Her questions came out like shots from those army guns you see on TV. Aunt Julia explained everything, including Mama's plan to call us at two o'clock.

Sunday glanced at the red and white Coca-Cola clock on the wall. "You've got time for iced tea, then. I made it fresh this morning. Garnet, you want a Nehi? I'm all out of Coke."

Sunday dumped a package of chocolate chip cookies onto a plate, fixed two glasses of tea, and handed me a cold bottle of grape soda. I was so thirsty I drank half

of it in one long swallow, until I saw Aunt Julia frowning. Then I set the bottle down and dabbed my mouth
with a paper napkin that had pumpkins and Pilgrims
printed on it.

"Those were left over from last Thanksgiving,"
Sunday explained. "A napkin is a napkin, the way I see
it. No sense in letting it go to waste." She munched on
a cookie and washed it down with iced tea. "So,
Garnet, how do you like Willow Flats?"

Aunt Julia saved me from telling a lie. "She just got
here. She hasn't had time to form an opinion."

"You'll like it once you get to know people,"
Sunday said to me. "Ours is a real friendly little town,
wouldn't you say so, Julia?"

The minute hand on the clock jerked up toward
two o'clock, and my stomach got tight. Sunday and
Aunt Julia talked on and on, but their voices seemed
far away. I stared at the phone like I could make it ring
just by looking at it.

At five after two, Aunt Julia checked her watch.
"Don't worry, Garnet. She'll call any second now."

At ten past, Sunday poured more tea. "Maybe
your mama's watch is slow," she said. "Or the clock
is fast."

"That's probably it," Aunt Julia said, but she didn't
sound convinced. "Maybe Melanie is waiting her turn
for the phone."

"In a hotel full of women, she might have quite a

wait," Sunday said. "We're the talkers of the species, no lie. Why, if communication were left up to the men of the world, Bell Telephone would go bankrupt from lack of revenue! More cookies, Garnet?"

I couldn't talk for the lump in my throat. I felt my heart harden against Mama a little more, building up one layer at a time, the way a pearl grows from a single grain of sand.

Then the phone rang, and my anger evaporated like fog in sunshine. Sunday grabbed the receiver, barked, "Larson's!" and handed the phone to my aunt.

"Melanie?" Aunt Julia said. "You had us worried. You said two o'clock. . . . Yes, I know, but . . . but . . ." She listened for a while, nodding her head. When Mama stopped for breath, Aunt Julia finally told her about Daddy's accident, and the hospital burn unit, and how no one was allowed to visit him until he was out of danger.

"You're his next of kin," Aunt Julia told her. "I'm sorry about your audition for those big record producers, but you'll have to go down there and sign the papers so the doctors can continue treating him. This is one time I can't bail you out, Melanie. It's your responsibility to look after your husband."

She listened some more. "At least the company is paying the medical bills. And there'll be disability checks for the girls until Duane is back on his feet." She frowned, sighed, and said, "Garnet wants to talk to you."

She handed me the phone and my mouth went dry. I swallowed. "Hello, Mama."

"Garnet? Baby? Is Opal there too? How are my precious gems?"

"Opal has a headache."

"She'll live. Listen, honey. Great news. Remember that clipping I showed you? The one about the producers looking for new talent? Well, I went over there this morning, and they gave me an appointment to sing one of my songs! Isn't that fabulous?"

The bottom of my stomach dropped out. What if Daddy was wrong about her talent, and she got herself a contract? Then she'd never ever come back. Still, if you really loved somebody, didn't you want what they wanted? Finally I said, "I guess so."

"You guess so? Can't you be just a little bit happy for me, or is that too much to ask?"

"Daddy needs you. Opal and I need you too. School starts in a couple of weeks and we want to go home."

"Well, just think about how ridiculous that sounds. If I took you to Mirabeau, who would look after you while I'm in New Orleans with your daddy?"

"We're not babies. We can stay by ourselves. Or I could stay with Jean Ann and Opal could stay with Linda. Or you could get Mrs. Streeter to stay with us. Please, Mama."

"I'm not about to foist you off onto the neighbors. You belong with family. When your daddy is better, and I'm on my feet in Nashville, I'll come back for you, like I promised. But for now you'll just have to be patient."

"But what about school? You said you'd come for us so we could start the year up there."

"I said I'd *try*. Who could predict your Daddy would get himself nearly killed and mess up everything? I swear, sometimes I think he pulls these stunts just to spite me."

In the background a woman hollered, "Will you hurry up with that phone?"

Mama said, "Listen. I've got to go. You be good, Garnet. Now let me talk to Julia again."

And that is how, on the following Saturday, Opal and I found ourselves standing in our underwear in the dressing room at Herman's Department Store, buying clothes for school in Willow Flats.

CHAPTER SIX

We each got two skirts and two blouses, and then we went to the shoe department, where a major battle ensued. Me and Opal wanted black ballerina flats like the ones in the teen magazines, but Aunt Julia picked up a brown, thick-soled oxford, a junior version of the clodhoppers she wore, and told the salesman we'd take two pair.

"But they're ugly!" I blurted.

"They are beyond ugly," Opal said. "They are truly hideous."

"Practical is what they are," Aunt Julia said. "You'll appreciate them when the snow flies."

"I won't wear them," Opal said. "You can't make me."

"Me either," I said. "I'll wear my sandals, even if I have outgrown them."

"Garnet's feet grow faster than kudzu," Opal said helpfully.

Aunt Julia blew out a long breath and held me with an icy stare. "For five cents I'd let you wear sandals all winter just to teach you a lesson. But the child welfare people would be on me like white on rice."

The salesman made a make-up-your-mind sound in his throat.

"Fine," Aunt Julia said with a wave of her hand. "Get whatever you want. Just don't come whining to me when your toes turn black from frostbite."

Me and Opal tried on the flats quickly, before Aunt Julia could change her mind. When we finished, she marched us across the store and made us try on winter coats.

"But it's a hundred degrees outside," I said.

"Cold weather will be here before you know it," Aunt Julia said. "Now's the time for the best selection. Besides, we'll need time to pay them off."

"You don't have enough money to pay for them?" Opal looked mortified.

The saleslady turned her back and pretended not to hear.

"When the oil company gets your daddy's disability checks started, we'll be fine," Aunt Julia said. "In the meantime, every penny counts. We'll put the coats on layaway for now."

I picked out a red coat with a white rabbit collar. Opal chose a black one with gold buttons.

"That's too old for you, Opal," Aunt Julia said. "Choose something else."

Opal twirled around, studying her reflection in the mirror. "I like this one."

"You're fourteen." Aunt Julia plucked another coat off the rack. "Try this one."

"I hate green."

The saleslady cleared her throat and took another coat off the rack. "Perhaps this one?" she said to Opal. "Navy is very popular this year, and this one is styled just like Doris Day's."

"Really?"

"Oh yes. I saw her new movie just last week. She looked divine. And the color does wonderful things for your blue eyes. I think you should seriously consider it."

Aunt Julia didn't say a word. After her crushing defeat at the Battle of the Shoes, she had figured out that her endorsement was the kiss of death. Opal tried on the navy coat and studied herself in the mirror. Finally she said, "I still like the black one better, but I'll take it."

While Aunt Julia and the saleslady did the paperwork, Opal and I went to the jewelry department. I tried on a gold circle pin like one I'd seen in the magazines. I wanted it real bad, but I knew better than to ask for it. Aunt Julia paid the saleslady two dollars to hold our coats, then we took our shopping bags and started down the street to the drugstore to wait for Sunday Larson, who had driven us to town in her truck.

The door to the pool hall was open. Inside it was dark as a cave except for red neon signs advertising beer. A bunch of boys in jeans and white T-shirts were playing pool at the table nearest the door. I caught a whiff of tobacco, hair tonic, and something sharp I figured was beer. As we walked past, one of the boys let out a long whistle and yelled, "Hey, Blondie!"

The other boys came to the door with their cue sticks in hand. "Hey, sweet thang!" one called. "What's your name?"

Opal tossed her hair and smiled like Marilyn Monroe at a movie premiere.

"Opal, stop it!" Aunt Julia grabbed my sister's arm and dragged her toward the drugstore so fast Opal had to jog to keep up. "Those Judd boys are nothing but trouble."

"How do you know?"

"I have lived my whole life in this town and know practically everybody. None of those boys are from good families."

"They seem perfectly nice to me," Opal said.

"Perfectly nice boys don't shout at girls in the

street, and they don't waste their lives hanging out in pool halls."

"Why not? There's nothing else to do in this stupid town. I myself am bored senseless."

"Me too," I said. "My brain is practically turning to mush."

Aunt Julia sighed. "If you're bored, you have no one to blame but yourself. You were both invited to the young people's hayrides at church."

"I'd rather be boiled in oil than spend Saturday night with a bunch of Bible-thumping losers." Opal wrenched her arm free. "You are so old-fashioned! In case you haven't noticed, this is 1960. Boys don't come a-sparkin' in the front parlor anymore."

"Maybe not, but they should!" Aunt Julia said, as if that were the last word on the subject. She peered down the street. "I wish Sunday would hurry up."

We waited and waited. The curb was so hot my shoes were practically melting into the concrete. "Let's wait inside the drugstore," I said.

"Keep your shirt on," Aunt Julia said. "I'm sure Sunday'll be along in a minute."

"We can go in where it's cool and I'll watch for her through the window."

A man pushed the door open. A thread of coolness, and part of a Conway Twitty song playing on the jukebox, came out with him. The voice of Mama's favorite singer brought back the caved-in feeling I'd had in the pit of my stomach the day she left. I felt queasy inside, like the time I threw up in Mama's pickup. I dug around in the shopping bag, took the lid off my shoe box, and fanned my face with it. "Why *can't* we go inside?" I asked.

Aunt Julia clamped her lips together and squeezed her eyes shut like she was adding up big numbers in her head. "Sunday had some business at the feed store. She's doing us a favor, Garnet. It wouldn't be polite to make her wait."

Then Sunday's pickup rounded the corner, the bed piled high with crates of live chickens. She screeched to a halt at the curb and grinned at us through the open window. "Sorry about the chickens. Albert had a sale on, and I couldn't resist. Julia, you can squeeze in up here next to my sacks of feed. I saved the girls a spot in back." She slapped her hand against the truck door. "Hop in!"

Opal shot Aunt Julia a murderous look, which Aunt Julia ignored. She got in beside Sunday and four sacks of chicken feed, placed her pocketbook on her lap, and gently closed the door like she was the Queen of England and Sunday's truck was her own personal limousine come to take her to Buckingham Palace. There was nothing me and Opal could do but climb into the back with the chickens.

Sunday leaned out the window and hollered, "All set, girls?"

Opal ducked her head and muttered, "Let's just go!"

We rattled down Main Street and went through the

stoplight just as it turned from green to yellow. Then we were on the blacktop and the truck picked up speed. Me and Opal hunkered down in the back, our hair whipping in the wind, dust and chicken feathers clogging our throats.

Just before we got to the turnoff to Aunt Julia's, a black car came barreling up behind us. It was the Judd boys from the pool hall. The driver honked as he sped around us. Two girls in the backseat laughed. One of them stuck her head out the window and yelled, "Cock-a-doodle-do!"

Opal scrunched down even farther and hid her face. "What a fabulous first impression. Those are probably the most popular kids in this entire town. I wish I were dead."

Sunday pulled into the yard. We grabbed our stuff and jumped out of the truck. Aunt Julia got out, then leaned her head in the open window and said to Sunday, "Thanks for the lift."

"Any time." Sunday ground the gears. "I'll see you girls bright and early Tuesday morning. Don't be late for your first day of school!"

Opal stared after the truck like a zombie in a horror movie. "Please tell me this is all a nightmare."

We started up the steps. "What are you talking about, Opal?" Aunt Julia asked.

"Please tell me I do not have to ride to school in a chicken truck."

"You do not have to ride to school in a chicken truck. Sunday drives the school bus. She usually passes by here around seven thirty, but we should be out at the mailbox by twenty after, just to be on the safe side."

"You're going with us?" I asked.

"Yes, to get you registered. Even in a town as small as Willow Flats, you can't just show up with no papers and start school."

"Mama has our records," I said. "Our report cards and everything."

Aunt Julia picked up Mozart, pushed open the door, and switched on the fan. "Take your new things upstairs and I'll get supper started."

We went up to our room, dumped everything on our beds, and changed from our skirts and blouses into shorts and T-shirts. I stared out the window at Aunt Julia's whirligigs, missing the good times Opal and I had had back home, shopping for new school stuff with Mama. Back then I could hardly wait for the first day of school, but now I was about as excited as a convict heading for the big house. Opal flopped onto her bed, folded herself up like a lawn chair, and stared at the wall. I could tell she was missing Mama too, but she wouldn't have admitted it if you tortured her. The weight of her hurt pushed down on me, but there was nothing I could say to make her feel better. Since Mama's phone call from Nashville, we hadn't talked about her much.

"Girls!" Aunt Julia called. "Come and eat!"

We had cold fried chicken, potato salad, and chocolate cake, a meal that I normally like a lot, but I was too homesick to enjoy any of it. Afterward we helped Aunt Julia with the dishes and then listened to the Dodgers game on the radio. Sandy Koufax was pitching. Like me, he batted right and threw left, and also like me, he was having a terrible year. The regular season was winding down, and Sandy's record was six games won and eleven lost.

When the game ended, Aunt Julia stood up and announced she was ready for bed.

"Don't stay up too late," she told us. "Church tomorrow."

Opal groaned. "It's our last Sunday before school starts. Do we have to go?"

After Opal's remark about the Bible-thumping losers, and her argument with Aunt Julia about the pool hall boys, I expected our aunt to insist that we go, but she surprised me. "All right. You can skip tomorrow," she said. "But don't go thinking you'll make a habit of it."

"No, ma'am," we said together.

We went upstairs and took out the Madame Fortuna game Opal had found that morning in a box at the back of Mama's closet. There was a fake crystal ball and a deck of cards the dealer shuffled before looking into the ball and asking a question. Then the other players drew a card that had the answer printed on it. The box said Madame Fortuna's cards had never been known to fail. I was dying to try it out. We sat cross-legged on the floor, the crystal ball between us.

"What should we ask?" Opal shuffled the cards.

"Ask if we'll ever see Mirabeau again," I said.

Opal gazed into the crystal ball. "Oh, Madame Fortuna, your humble servant Garnet wishes to know: Will she ever see her beloved hometown again?"

I passed my hands back and forth over the cards, waiting until it felt right before I pulled one out of the deck. I turned it over.

MAYBE.

"That tells us nothing." Opal shuffled the cards again and asked another question: "Oh, Madame Fortuna, does Waymon Harris like me?"

DEFINITELY.

Opal laughed, and her face turned pink, even though it was just a dumb game. She passed the cards to me. "Your turn to be the dealer."

I shuffled the cards and gazed into the crystal ball. "Madame Fortuna, will my daddy get well?"

Opal drew a card and turned it over. UNCERTAIN.

"This is stupid," I said. "It doesn't answer anything!"

"Try one more," Opal said.

I shuffled the cards and spoke again to the crystal ball. "Will Mama come back?"

Opal chose a card. Turned it over.

UNCERTAIN.

CHAPTER SEVEN

"Which one looks best?" Opal stood at the mirror in her underwear, holding both her new blouses. "I can't decide."

It was barely light outside, but in our bedroom the air was already so hot the paint was practically peeling off the bedposts. A trickle of sweat slid down my backbone. I smoothed my skirt and combed my hair for the third time, my stomach jumpy with first-day-of-school nerves. Back home I knew girls whose clothes were the wrong style, girls who lived in the wrong part of town. Everybody treated them like trash, even when they weren't. I didn't want to make a mistake and turn out like them.

"It doesn't matter," I told Opal. "You'd look beautiful in a tow sack."

"Be serious," she said. "We have to go in looking perfect."

"Girls!" Aunt Julia hollered from the bottom of the stairs. "Breakfast is getting cold, and the bus will be here in twenty minutes."

"I'm not hungry!" I yelled back.

Aunt Julia climbed the stairs and came into our room. "You can't skip breakfast. Go to school on an empty stomach and the whole day will start off wrong."

"It's already starting off wrong," I said. "Look at my hair! It hangs down like a spaniel's ears."

"It looks very nice," Aunt Julia said. "And that blouse looks pretty on you too."

Getting a compliment on my looks was such a novelty I couldn't think of anything to say, even though I realized Aunt Julia was only trying to calm my nerves.

Opal decided on a black skirt and a red shirt that had little black swirls on it. She zipped her skirt, pulled her hair into a ponytail, and dug through her drawer for a bracelet. She picked up her new bottle of My Sin, then put it down again, as if opening it in Willow Flats would be the same as admitting we were never going home.

We picked up our new notebooks and followed Aunt Julia to the kitchen, which smelled like fried ham and biscuits. Despite my jitters, I was suddenly hungry. Even Opal couldn't resist Aunt Julia's biscuits. She ate two with grape jelly and reached for a third. "These are good."

"I've been cooking since your mama was a baby,"

Aunt Julia said. "Back then my biscuits would barely support life. I like to think I've improved some since then."

Then the bus rumbled down the road. The horn blared.

"Sunday's here!" Aunt Julia glanced at the clock. "And it's only a quarter after. Go brush your teeth. I'll wait for you in the bus."

When we got out to the bus, Aunt Julia was sitting right behind the driver's seat talking to Sunday. "There you are," Sunday said. "Hop aboard."

The bus reeked of old gym shoes and gasoline. Me and Opal were the first ones on the bus, so we had our choice of seats. We sat behind Aunt Julia. Sunday stomped on the gas and we headed down the road. We passed Charlie's place, a log cabin nestled in a grove of trees. A wooden canoe and a paddle were propped against the porch.

We passed Sunday's store and the Texaco, and Reverend Underwood's church. Sunday turned onto a red dirt road that ran beside a fenced pasture and stopped in front of a run-down yellow house that made Aunt Julia's place look like Buckingham Palace. Three barefoot girls waited at the gate.

"Them's the Barton girls," Sunday said. "They don't talk much."

She cranked the door open. The girls climbed onto the bus, gave me and Opal a good looking-over, then took seats at the back. Opal opened her notebook, took out a pen, and hunched over so I couldn't see what she was writing. We rumbled up one road and down the other and the bus filled up, mostly with kids too young to drive or too poor to own a car. Nobody said a word to Opal and me, but there were plenty of nosy stares. I leaned over to talk to my sister, but she was frowning, writing furiously, so I left her alone.

Finally we got to the schoolhouse. The bus chugged up a long driveway and shuddered to a stop. Everybody poured out in a gust of talk and keyed-up laughter. The little kids raced across the road to their school. Aunt Julia smoothed her skirt and picked up her pocketbook off the seat. "I won't be long," she said to Sunday.

We walked up the steps past a knot of boys wearing tight jeans, white T-shirts, and Elvis haircuts. A bunch of girls in ponytails and matching outfits stood whispering together. I thought about Jean Ann and all our plans for starting seventh grade together, and my eyes went blurry.

Inside, we walked down a dark hallway that smelled of lemon floor wax and chalk. We passed rows of gray metal lockers and a glass trophy case decorated with red and white streamers and a poster that said WELCOME BACK, WARRIORS! Red poster board arrows outlined with gold glitter pointed one way to the seventh- and eighth-grade wing, the other to the high school classrooms. We went into the office.

"Good morning!" the secretary said to Aunt Julia. She wore a beehive hairdo and a name tag that said IDA WINK, OFFICE. "How may I help you?"

Aunt Julia explained that we were there to register for school, since we were staying with her while our mama was away on business and our daddy was in the hospital in New Orleans.

"I saw his name on the prayer list at my church last week," Ida said to me. "As long as the Lord has ahold of your daddy, he'll be all right."

She reached inside a drawer and gave Aunt Julia a bunch of papers to fill out. Aunt Julia unzipped her purse and handed Ida Wink the thick envelope Mama had given her the day she'd dumped us in Willow Flats. Ida opened it and all our report cards, shot records, test scores, everything, fell out. Opal shot me a white-hot look and the truth sank in. Mama had never intended to come for us at all, and Aunt Julia knew it all the time. I felt far away, like I was standing on a piece of the planet that had broken apart from the rest of the universe. I squeezed my eyes shut, trying to pretend none of it was happening. It was all I could do to keep from crying while Ida gave us our schedules and told us where our lockers were and how to get to the cafeteria.

She dumped a load of books in my arms. "Here you go. English is your first-period class, and your homeroom as well. Your other classes are math, history, health and gym, and art." She handed me a slip of yellow paper. "Here's the combination to your locker. Don't lose it."

Then she piled a stack of ninth-grade books on the counter for Opal and repeated her warning about the locker combination. Opal said, "Should we swallow it so the Commies can't get it?"

"Opal," Aunt Julia said in her warning voice.

Ida Wink frowned. "I guess you haven't heard that the Russians who shot down our pilot over there just threw him in jail for ten years. I wouldn't joke about Communists if I were you. They're dangerous people."

The bell rang.

"Time for class," Ida said. "Don't be late. And welcome! I'm sure you'll both be true Willow Flats Warriors in no time!"

Aunt Julia started to speak, but I was so mad I turned away and pretended to study my schedule. Opal picked up her books and stalked to the door. Before she could open it, a boy rushed in, nearly knocking us both down. Opal's armload of books tumbled to the floor.

"Sorry!" the boy said.

Opal scooped up her books and tried to grab her notebook before I could see what she'd written during our bus ride. But she was too late. The whole page was filled with a single sentence in her small, neat handwriting.

I hate Melanie Hubbard.

CHAPTER EIGHT

By the time I found my way to English class, the only empty seat was in the front row by the window. I slid into my chair and opened my book like I couldn't wait to learn all about adjectives and prepositions.

Without a teacher in the room, chaos reigned. People were standing on chairs, yelling back and forth, throwing spit wads. A couple of boys at the back of the room were sharing a comic book and laughing. A girl in a blue dress two sizes too small ripped a page out of her book and used it to blot her lipstick. Two rows behind me sat one of the sad-eyed Barton girls, and Cooley, the bristly-haired boy from Aunt Julia's church known only by his last name. He was on his hands and knees, tying another boy's shoelaces to the legs of his chair, stopping only long enough to push his slipping-down glasses back onto his nose.

Somebody called my name. I turned and Faith Underwood, the preacher's redheaded daughter, mouthed, "Hi." I tried not to show my surprise when I said hi back. Then the door opened and the room went quiet as a graveyard. The teacher charged in, dropped her books on the desk, picked up a piece of chalk, and wrote on the blackboard in fancy curling script, *Miss Lillian Sparrow, Seventh Grade English.*

Miss Sparrow looked the opposite of her name. She was tall and muscled like a baseball player. She wore round tortoiseshell glasses, a short, spiky haircut, and a no-nonsense expression that reminded me of Mrs. Streeter, our neighbor back in Mirabeau. Behind her back, Mama referred to Mrs. Streeter as Old Starch and Vinegar. The name fit Miss Sparrow perfectly.

She spun around and dusted the chalk off her fingers. "Anybody in the wrong room?"

When nobody moved, she opened a grade book like the ones the teachers in Mirabeau used, and started calling the roll. When she finished, she peered at me over the top of her glasses. "I know almost everybody around here, but I don't recognize your name. You must be new."

"Yes, ma'am."

She nodded, stood up straight, like she was being measured for a new suit of clothes, and started reading off her rules in a voice that made them sound as if they had been handed down from heaven on a stone tablet:

> No talking unless you are called upon.
> No running inside the classroom or in the hallways.
> No gum chewing permitted at any time.
> Late homework will not be accepted without a note from your parents.

When she finished with the rules, she handed out an assignment sheet and told us how to put a heading on our papers. We were commanded to write only in blue ink, to fold homework assignments in half lengthwise when we handed them in, and not to rip pages from a spiral notebook because she hated ragged edges.

"Any questions?" Her gaze went all around the room and stopped when it landed on Cooley. "Cooley. Untie Nathan's shoelaces this instant, and see me after class."

Cooley cackled like a mad scientist in a horror movie, but he minded Starch and Vinegar all the same. Then we settled down to read our first assignment, *The Ransom of Red Chief*. When the bell rang, ending the class, I gathered up my stuff and started down the hall. Faith Underwood caught up with me outside the gym.

"How's it going, Garnet?"

I shrugged.

"First days are tough," Faith said. "But now that you've met Miss Sparrow, the worst is over. She's the terror of the whole seventh-grade faculty. Who do you have next period?"

I took out my schedule, wondering why Faith had taken a sudden interest in my welfare. At church she and her sister had hung around with their own friends and spoken to me only when their daddy was watching.

Faith peered over my shoulder. "Uh-oh. Mr. Stanley for math. People say he's not as mean as he looks, but don't cross him. He's got a memory like an elephant's."

She shifted her books to her other arm. "Oh, you lucky thing! You got Paula Mendez for art. She's new this year, and everybody in town says she's an honest-to-Pete bohemian!"

I had no idea what a bohemian was, but I nodded enthusiastically. A bohemian. Lucky me.

"And that's not all," Faith said. "My daddy saw an exhibit of her work in Fort Worth last spring, and he says her art is all about people fighting the government. He says she may even be a Communist."

Remembering what Ida Wink had just said about Communists being dangerous, I didn't figure they'd let one inside the school.

"My mother says it's just plain odd for a woman to be more interested in politics than in having a husband," Faith declared. "So Mother enrolled me in home ec instead. She says every girl should know how to cook and sew."

The tardy bell rang.

"Listen," Faith said, "I have to go, but I'll meet you for lunch if you want. Bye!"

She ran for her class and I went to math. Mr. Stanley took roll and then handed out a sheet of story problems. I read the first one and my stomach clenched. The Math Problem from H-e-double-l was about trains that start from New York and Los Angeles at different times going at different speeds, and I was supposed to figure out what time they would pass each other on the tracks in Chicago. We'd had similar problems in sixth grade back home. I knew the answer involved lots of x's and y's plus all the time zones, but I never could figure it out. In the space for writing the answer, I put "Consult the timetable" and went on to the next problem, an easier one where you had to convert square feet into square yards.

Then it was time for art class. I found a seat at a table in the back just as the bohemian swept in. She was tiny, shorter than Opal, and dressed in a paint-spattered smock over a pair of wide-legged pants, black suede boots, and an armful of silver bracelets that jingled when she moved.

She scribbled her name on the chalkboard and waited until we were quiet. Then she said, "Good morning! I am Paula Mendez."

In her soft Spanish accent it came out sounding like "Pow-la," and that is how I thought of her from then on.

"Together we will learn what it means to be an artist. And so, a question. What is the purpose of art?"

When nobody volunteered, she consulted her class list and said, "Lee Crockett?"

A boy behind me said, "I don't care."

"Really? Then why are you in this class?"

"Shop class was full."

"I see." She looked at her list again. "Susan Mallory. What is the purpose of art?"

"To make something that's beautiful?" Susan opened her compact and checked her lipstick.

"Perhaps," Miss Mendez said, "but not always in the way we usually think of beauty." She dimmed the lights and switched on a slide projector. The machine whirred and a picture appeared on the screen at the front of the room. The image wasn't like anything I'd ever seen, except maybe on the cover of a superhero comic book. One part of the picture, mostly painted in dark reds and deep purples, showed a man lying on his back, injured by a big machine. The second part showed women with flowers, fruit, and round-faced children gathered together, and in the third part all of them were marching off together.

Without turning on the light, Powla said, "*Now* who has an idea about the purpose of art?"

"It tells a story." I was so engrossed in the picture I didn't realize I'd said anything until I heard my words floating in the air.

"Yes. The story we see here is the story of man being oppressed, imprisoned by a machine."

The projector whirred, the screen went blank, and then another picture came up. It was not beautiful, but I couldn't stop looking at the images of an Indian on a cross and, above it, a huge American eagle.

"Government can also be an oppressor of people," Powla said, "as this mural by David Siqueiros clearly shows. Why do you think the artist called it *Tropical America*? Mr. Crockett? Any ideas?"

"I don't know."

"Well, let's think about it. What does 'tropical' mean?"

"Like in the jungle or something?"

"If we wanted to go to someplace tropical from here in the United States, which direction would we go?"

Somebody else said, "South?"

"Exactly," Powla said. "And so, *Tropical America* might be another name for . . ."

"Mexico?" Lee guessed.

"Excellent." Powla turned the projector off, switched the lights on, and perched on the corner of her desk. "David Siqueiros is a very famous Mexican muralist. In his piece called *Tropical America,* he wanted to show that his people and their land were exploited by their neighbors to the north; namely, the Americans, as symbolized by the eagle perched above the man on the cross. In his view the best art says something about man and society. So even though you may not think of these pictures as pretty, they are beautiful in their sentiment, and in the passion with which the artist expresses himself."

She took a copy of *Tropical America* from a storage cabinet and tacked it to the wall. "This year we will learn more about this man, Siqueiros, and about other muralists who share his view that art should be created to express a national experience rather than for the artist's personal satisfaction. For now, though, let's see what you can do."

She handed out tubes of oil paint, sets of watercolors, bottles of India ink, stacks of canvas, plastic, and wood, and we experimented by painting on a bunch of different surfaces while she walked around making encouraging comments, even when the pictures were awful.

"Hmm," she murmured when she saw my painting of my house on Piney Road. "Your proportion is a bit off, and this picture doesn't say anything important yet, but you have a fine eye for form and color." She leaned down to read my signature in the corner. Her perfume smelled like Mama's gardenias, and for a minute I couldn't think.

"Well, Garnet," Powla said. "I believe you show real promise."

I didn't know whether she was just being nice or whether it was true. I hoped it was true, but so far nobody had seen anything special about me. At the end of sixth grade, the junior high counselors in Mirabeau had held a big meeting and told us how important it was to explore a lot of different subjects in seventh grade. They said the talents we developed in junior high would carry over into our adult lives. I had learned to draw and paint a little. I could throw a decent fastball. But I wasn't sure how these skills would be useful later on.

I finished my picture and left it on the drying table, then went to the restroom to wash my hands. Faith Underwood was standing at the sink with her back to the door, talking to someone I couldn't see. Before she saw me, I ducked into a stall that smelled like disinfectant.

"Honestly, Faith, I can't be your friend anymore if you're going to hang around with that Garnet girl," said a voice. "What a strange name! She's such a little mouse. And she's plain as a mud fence. Too bad she didn't get her older sister's good looks."

Even though I knew it was true, even though I had said it a thousand times to myself, it hurt to hear somebody else say it out loud. My throat ached. It wasn't fair that Opal was pretty and popular and I was such a loser. The taste of envy burned hot and sour on my tongue.

Faith said, "Relax, will you? Her aunt goes to my daddy's church, and I promised to be nice to the new kid today. It's not as if I really like her or anything."

Then she turned the water on and I couldn't hear anything except laughter. When they left, I came out of the stall and washed the paint off my fingers. The bell rang and I found my way to the cafeteria, even though my stomach felt so tight I thought I'd throw up.

I got in line behind a couple of girls wearing matching red jumpers and white blouses. One of them turned around. "I haven't seen you here before," she said, her eyes wide and judging. "Where are you from?"

The line moved. The lady behind the steam table said to the girl, "Chicken or beef?" saving me from having to answer. When it was my turn, I asked for chicken, and she filled my tray with a gray substance that might have been either chicken or beef, then added a spoonful of mushy green beans and a blob of peach cobbler. I looked around for a seat.

It was only the first day, but already I could see which tables were reserved for the people everybody liked and which ones belonged to the kids at the bottom of the popularity chart. At one end of the reject table, two of the Barton sisters hunched over their sausage-and-biscuit sack lunches. A chubby girl in a red sweater too heavy for the weather, and a couple of pimply-faced boys in overalls and work boots, sat across from them. Except for the Bartons, I didn't know any of their names, but I knew their kind. Every school has kids like them. Kids who wear the same clothes all year, who smell funny, who look scared and lost, or tough and defiant.

I walked past the table and nobody even looked up. A cloud of gloom hung above them because they knew what was ahead—179 more days just as miserable as the first.

"There you are!" Faith said, coming up beside me. She jerked her head toward the blond goddess standing beside her. "Garnet, this is Celestial Jones. Our daddies went to preacher school together. We've been friends since kindergarten."

"Hi," said the girl in a voice I recognized from the restroom. "Come sit with us today."

Go ahead and call me a hypocrite for sitting with them, knowing they really didn't want me, but I just couldn't sit with the other losers on the very first day of school. I followed Faith and Celestial to an empty table near the door. They sat beside each other, their shoulders touching in that best-friend kind of way. I took a seat across from them. Pretty soon the table filled with other girls wearing gold circle collar pins and tortoise-shell head bands.

"Hey, everybody," Celestial said, waving her fork in my direction. "This is Garnet Hubbard. She's new."

They stared at me like I was a six-legged cow in a freak show. A couple of them smiled, but then they all went back to their own conversations. I pushed my food around on my tray, trying not to remember it was the first day of school in Mirabeau, too.

The cafeteria doors opened and the ninth graders thundered in. I spotted Opal right away. She rushed through the serving line and took a seat right in the middle of the prettiest girls in ninth grade. She tossed her head and teased the boy who had nearly knocked her down in the office, wrinkled her nose at the cafeteria food, laughed with the boys from the pool hall about Sunday Larson's chicken truck, making a joke out of the whole experience before they could laugh at her. It was amazing how she was born knowing the secret code of the popular kids, a code I couldn't crack.

I ate a couple of bites of cobbler. The milk had gone lukewarm in the carton. Faith and Celestial were ignoring me, talking about some program at church I was not a part of, proving to the rest of the table that I didn't really belong with them. I got up to empty my tray.

One of the freshmen crossed his arms and stared at me until my neck prickled.

"Keep staring like that and you'll wear your eyes out," I said.

He stuck his legs out, blocking my way. "Where do you think you're going?" He grinned at the boy sitting next to him, and it made me mad.

"What's it to you?" I said.

"What's it tu yew?" he mocked. "What kind of hillbilly accent is that?"

His sidekick cracked up. Chocolate milk spurted out his nose and sprayed onto the table. I turned around to go the other way, but another boy slid his chair into the aisle.

"Are you one of those Louisiana swamp rats come up here to infest Oklahoma?" he asked.

"Get out of my way."

"Git out o' yore way? Okay, I will. But first I want to hear you talk some more. Say 'I'm a filthy Louisiana swamp rat' and I'll let you pass."

I picked up my milk carton and was about to dump the contents onto the cretin's head, but just then one of the coaches strolled by. "What's the trouble here, boys?"

"Nothing." The cretin moved his chair. I escaped to the garbage can, threw my food away, and ran outside. I turned the corner and there was Miss Mendez sitting on the back steps with a cigarette in her hand.

She blew out a thin stream of smoke and smiled. "Uh-oh. I'm busted. You won't tell on me, will you?"

I was so mad I couldn't say anything. Miss Mendez scooted over to make room for me on the steps, and ground her cigarette into the dirt. "You're Garnet, right? From third period?"

I nodded.

"First day here?"

"Yes, ma'am."

"Mine, too. God, what a backwater." She squinted at the washed-out Oklahoma sky. "My father had a heart attack this spring, and I came here to look after him. What's your excuse?"

I didn't feel like telling her the whole story, so I said that me and Opal were staying with my aunt while our mama looked for a place up in Nashville.

"Nashville's not a bad town, if you like your music chicken-fried. I prefer classical guitar. Do you know Segovia?"

"No, ma'am."

"He's one of the best guitarists in the world. I listened to him constantly when I studied in Spain."

We could hear the little kids yelling in their schoolyard across the road and the birds singing in the oak trees. She said, "Don't let them get you down, Garnet. It's the ignorant among us who are threatened by anyone or anything they don't understand."

"Yes, ma'am."

She stood up. "Lunch period's almost over. We'd better go, before the bell rings and we both get into trouble."

I went back inside. The ninth graders were still hovering around Opal. Most of the seventh graders had drifted away, but Celestial and Faith were sitting right where I'd left them, so busy chattering like Heckle and Jeckle, they hadn't even noticed I'd gone.

Ida Wink made a beeline for me. "Where have you been? Mr. Conley wants to see you."

Faith's eyes widened. "Gosh, Garnet, what did you

do to get sent to the principal's office on the very first day?"

"Mind your own business, Miss Underwood," said Ida. "Come along, Garnet."

I followed the secretary down the hall, my blood rushing loudly in my ears.

"In here," she said, motioning me into an office. To the man behind the desk, she said, "Mr. Conley? This is Garnet Hubbard."

Then she closed the door.

Mr. Conley waved me into a chair, folded his hands, and stared at me like a scientist studying a bug under a microscope. "So, Garnet, this is your first day with us."

"Yes, sir," I said to the portrait of George Washington on the wall behind his desk.

"Finding your way around all right?"

"Yes, sir."

"Any idea why I sent for you?"

"No, sir."

He handed me the sheet of math problems from Mr. Stanley's class. Somebody had drawn an angry red circle around the box where I'd written my answer to the train problem.

"'Consult the timetable,'" Mr. Conley said. "Does that sound like an appropriate answer to you, Garnet?"

"I couldn't figure it out! I'm no good in math. Besides, it's a stupid question."

"Come again?"

"Say you want to know what time the eight-ten train from Los Angeles gets into Chicago. You look it up in the timetable. You don't sit there with paper and pen, writing down stuff like x minus y plus ten divided by two equals z."

"That's hardly the point. The point is to teach you to think logically and to solve problems." Mr. Conley ran his hand over his egg-shaped head. "I agree that using a timetable is faster than working the answer out mathematically, but Mr. Stanley is highly offended. He feels you were being disrespectful."

"I wasn't!"

"Well, then. Apologize to him and we'll forget this ever happened."

"But I didn't do anything wrong!"

Mr. Conley let the seconds tick by until I thought my head would explode. Finally I said, "Okay! I'll apologize."

"Good." He handed me a hall pass and I escaped to history class, where I spent the whole period working on my apology to Mr. Stanley. But no matter how I said it, the words didn't seem right. I knew it was because I felt wronged, and in my heart I wasn't truly sincere. I finally wrote, *Dear Mr. Stanley, I'm sorry. Garnet Hubbard,* and put it in his mailbox in the office after fifth period.

Health class was as boring in Oklahoma as it was

back home. The teacher, Mr. Riley, was also our gym teacher and the coach for the ninth-grade basketball team. As proof of his important position, he carried a bunch of gym keys that rattled when he walked, and a stack of play diagrams, with x's and dotted lines to show where the ball should go.

He took roll, then made us sign up to do a report on some aspect of "Your Changing Body." We had our choice of the body's various systems. I picked the circulatory system, because the red and blue lines representing veins and arteries reminded me of the lines on Mama's road map. Maybe I hoped drawing a map of my heart would somehow help me find a way back into hers.

Mr. Riley collected our sign-up sheets and explained that during the year we'd study "Things That Are Bad for You," such as sneaking beer and smoking cigarettes, followed by "Good Health Habits" like washing your hands, covering your mouth when you sneeze, and looking both ways before you cross the street. Then he fired up his film projector, dimmed the lights, and worked on his basketball stuff while we watched a jerky film about traffic safety, even though none of us was old enough to drive.

Cooley and a couple of other boys sitting in the back row cracked jokes and laughed so loudly during the film that Mr. Riley had to yell at them twice to be quiet and listen.

It was a huge waste of time. What I really needed to

know was whether I would ever grow breasts like Opal's, what to do to make people like me, and how to convince Mama to come home. Maybe if Mr. Riley showed films about stuff like that, people would pay attention.

When the film ended, Mr. Riley marched us all outside and made us run laps around the building until we were red-faced and winded. Then we did a few stretching exercises to cool down and went back inside just as the final bell rang. I dumped everything into my locker and went out to catch the bus. Opal was standing on the steps with a couple dozen of her new best friends. She looked up and waved, but she didn't invite me over, so I left her alone. Soon the bus lumbered up the road and stopped in the driveway. I got on and took the seat behind Sunday. Opal sashayed down the aisle and sat across from a dark-haired girl who looked like she'd stepped out of a fashion magazine. The two Judd brothers from the pool hall got on. One sat with the fashion model, the other one sat with Opal.

We were halfway home when Opal let out a whoop so loud Sunday jammed on the brakes and yelled, "What's going on back there?"

I turned around. One of the Judds had his arms wrapped around Opal and was trying to kiss her. Opal was laughing and slapping his hands away, but not like she really meant for him to stop. The girl sitting across from Opal was kissing the other Judd, and half the bus was cheering them on.

"Hey, cut that out before I toss you all off this bus," Sunday hollered. "Opal, you and Travis break it up. Now!"

Travis let Opal go. She smoothed her hair and looked at him, and they both burst out laughing again. I was mortified.

It was a big relief when Sunday stopped at our house to let us off. She gave Opal a look that would stop a bullet, but my sister just waved and said, "See you tomorrow!"

"Who was that girl?" I asked as we crossed the road. "She looks like a model."

"Cheryl Winslow. She's a sophomore, but she's in my study hall."

Aunt Julia waved from the porch and started down the lane to meet us.

"Don't tell her about Travis, okay?" Opal shifted her armload of books and we headed for the mailbox. "We were just fooling around."

"If you keep acting like that with old Octopus Boy, Sunday will tell," I said. "I think it's disgusting."

Opal grinned. "You won't when you get older."

I opened the mailbox and took out the electric bill, the church newsletter, and a Sears flyer. Nothing from Mama.

Aunt Julia reached the mailbox. "How was your first day? Are your teachers nice? Did you make friends?"

"It was horrible." My anger at Aunt Julia was coming back, hot as road tar in August. "Everybody hates me, even the teachers." I pushed the mail into her hands and took off running.

"Wait!" Aunt Julia called, but I ran into the house and pounded up the stairs. I curled up on my bed and cried. Mozart waded through the covers and settled down next to me. The door opened and Aunt Julia came in. "Garnet, I want to talk to you."

I scratched Mozart's head and studied the wall like it was the most interesting thing I'd ever seen.

She perched on the edge of my bed. "I know this is hard for you," she began. "None of us asked for this situation, but now that it's here, we've got to try to make the best of it. I'm doing everything I can to make it work, but you have to try too."

"You lied to me! You knew from the start that Mama wasn't coming back before school started, and you didn't say one word."

Aunt Julia sighed. "I thought it best to let you get used to living here before I broke the news. Then your daddy got hurt and you were so upset I didn't have the heart to tell you. But I am sorry you feel betrayed."

"They all hate me." I told her about the boys in the cafeteria who called me a swamp rat even though I had never set foot in the state of Louisiana, and that I'd had to apologize to Mr. Stanley even though I hadn't done anything wrong.

"The first day in a new place is always hard," Aunt Julia said. "Give it some time. You'll make friends."

"I *have* friends," I said. "Back home in Mirabeau."

"Hey, Garnet!" Opal yelled from the bottom of the stairs. "Are you hungry?"

"Come on," Aunt Julia said. "I made a blueberry cobbler."

Like that would fix everything.

CHAPTER NINE

"All right, people, settle down!" Starch and Vinegar banged her fist on her desk until everybody stopped talking. It was the middle of October, one of those perfect blue and gold days that make you impatient to be outside. Brown leaves swirled past the window and settled into the bed of dying periwinkles out by the flagpole. A gaggle of geese heading south for the winter cut a black *V* in the sky. I doodled in my notebook, only half listening to Miss Sparrow.

"The cafeteria ladies have brought to our attention the fact that a great deal of food is being wasted each day," she said. "Yesterday I personally counted half a dozen unwrapped sandwiches, three whole apples, and five unopened cartons of milk tossed away." She shook her head like a person trying to understand quantum physics. "That much wasted food would wipe out hunger in Africa."

Her talk of sandwiches and fresh fruit made my mouth water. Aunt Julia hadn't received a penny of my daddy's disability money, even though Mr. Hancock had promised her the paperwork was done, and we had no money for anything. Our winter coats were still on layaway, Opal had to miss her class trip to the history museum in Tulsa because we couldn't afford the bus fare, and a hot lunch, or even a bologna sandwich made with store-bought bread, was out of the question. Instead, every day I brought sausage and biscuits that turned the paper sack greasy and made the inside of my locker smell like a diner. I doubted even a hungry kid in Ethiopia would touch it.

Miss Sparrow finished lecturing us about being wasteful, then collected money for the magic show assembly scheduled for that afternoon. I was the only one who didn't have the quarter it cost to watch a man in a cheap tuxedo pull colored scarves out of a hat. I really didn't mind not seeing the show. What I minded was being too poor to see it, and having everybody else know it.

Since arriving at Aunt Julia's, my life had become one big conglomeration of things I couldn't have and things I couldn't do. Even though I had apologized to Aunt Julia for getting mad at her on the first day of school, she hardly talked to me at all. Opal said Aunt

Julia was just preoccupied with getting Daddy's disability checks started, and I guess that was true, but it didn't explain why she let Opal do whatever she wanted but wouldn't let me do anything. When I asked her why, she said it was "because I said so." Like she would fall over dead if she had to give me a reason.

The eight thirty bell rang. Miss Sparrow sent Faith Underwood to the office with the magic-show money. Then she announced the annual costume day for Halloween. "No masks will be allowed," she said.

Cooley raised his hand. "How about face paint? I want to dress up like Frankenstein's monster."

"You're already a monster," said Nathan Brown.

"Boys." Miss Sparrow held up her hand for silence. "Face paint will be fine," she told Cooley. "But I do not want to see a repeat of the dried ketchup on your face from last year. That looked much too realistic. Poor Mrs. Wink was ready to summon the sheriff."

She answered a couple of other questions, then took up her copy of *To Kill a Mockingbird,* a book by Miss Harper Lee. Miss Sparrow was reading it to us one chapter a day, and I thought it was the best book in the world. Maybe it was because the kids in the story, Jem and Scout Finch, didn't have a mother either, and their daddy, Atticus, with his kind words and quiet ways, reminded me of my own daddy.

We were in health class when the time came for the

magic-show assembly. Everybody else went to the auditorium, and Mr. Riley sent me to the library. Darlene
Barton hadn't shown up for school that day, but her two
sisters were there, hunched over their books. A couple of
ninth-grade boys were tormenting the girl in the red
sweater I'd seen at lunch on day one. I took a seat by the
window and waited for Opal to come waltzing in and
make everything okay. She'd crack some joke that would
make it seem like we were the cool kids for skipping a
dumb magic show. But she never arrived. Eventually I
opened my book and pretended to read, but inside my
head I was yelling at Mama for messing up my life so bad.

The last bell rang just as the magic show ended. I
could hear applause and laughter coming from the
auditorium, and excited voices as the hallways filled.
Cooley came tearing into the library and asked the
librarian for a book on how to do magic tricks. I was
headed for the door when he said, "Hey, Garnet. What
are you going to be for Halloween?"

I kept walking. I was definitely not in the mood for
his wisecracks.

"Maybe you could dress up like Little Orphan
Annie, seeing as how your daddy's sick and your mama
ran off."

"She didn't run off. She's in Nashville getting a
record contract, and she's going to be more famous
than Cordell Jackson."

"That's not what I heard. I heard your mama

dropped you off like a stray cat and hightailed it out of Willow Flats before the sun went down."

I wasn't surprised he knew. Cooley's family, and the rest of them down at Aunt Julia's church, acted holier than Swiss cheese, but anytime they got wind of the tiniest piece of gossip, they were all over it like a hen on a June bug. "My mother loves me," I said. "That's why she named me for a precious gem."

Cooley cackled. "Garnets aren't precious gems."

"They are too."

"Bet me."

Through the library window, I saw Sunday Larson's bus coming up the road. "Forget it. I have to go."

I escaped to the bus and took my usual seat behind Sunday.

"How's it going, Garnet?" she asked. "Any word from your mama lately?"

"I wish everybody would just shut up about my mother!"

Sunday blinked. "Well, pardon me for breathing."

She ground the gears and honked at a couple of boys standing in the driveway. Then the ninth graders burst through the schoolhouse doors and boarded the bus. I scooted over, hoping Opal would see that I'd had a bad day and would sit with me, but she passed me by like a freight train passing a hobo and sat in the back with Seth Naylor, the human scarecrow who'd nearly knocked her over in the office on the first day of school. Seth's dishwater-colored hair was falling into his eyes, and a pimple the size of Cleveland was forming on his chin. His arms and legs stuck out at weird angles, and his Adam's apple bobbed up and down when he talked. All in all he was fairly pathetic, but Opal was looking at him like he was first prize in a raffle she couldn't believe she'd won. It amazed me what she found attractive.

The bus jostled over the bumps and potholes in the road as we passed Charlie Twelvetrees's place. He was in the yard puttering around his canoe. When Sunday tooted the horn, Charlie looked up and waved.

"He sure takes good care of that canoe," I said, hoping Sunday would understand I meant it as an apology for my outburst.

"He takes it to the river every day, and he's way past eighty." She stopped at our mailbox. "One of these days we'll find him dead out there. Stubborn old goat." She cranked open the bus door. "Take it easy, Garnet."

I waited for Opal to get off the bus. "Where were you during the magic show?" I demanded. Sunday gunned the engine and took off up the road. "I had to sit in the library with the Bartons."

"Seth paid for my ticket." Opal shook out her hair. "He's shy, but nice."

"What about Octopus Boy? And Waymon Harris? I thought you were *his* girlfriend."

Opal looked so upset I wished I hadn't brought up the subject of the boy she'd left behind. "We'll never go back to Mirabeau," she said as we crossed the road to the mailbox. "And Waymon has forgotten me. He never answered my letter."

Jean Ann hadn't answered my letter either. As far as our friends back home were concerned, me and Opal might as well be dead. I opened Aunt Julia's mailbox and pulled out a huge brown envelope covered in postage stamps. "Holy smokes! It's from Mama!"

"Let me see!" Opal dropped her books and ripped open the envelope. A note fluttered out.

> *My Precious Gems,*
>
> *I hope you like these presents. The shirt is for you, Garnet. The swimsuit is for Opal. It's the very latest style from Paris. I miss you both and I'll be there to get you very soon. Cross my heart.*
>
> *Love, Mama*

Deep down I didn't think Mama's promise could be for real—look at how many times she had disappointed me already—but I wanted to believe it like it was the truest thing I'd ever heard. Opal unfolded the swimsuit, two scraps of bright yellow fabric with seahorses printed on it. "It's a bikini!" She started to laugh. "It's just like Mama to send a swimsuit when it's too cold to wear it. As if I'd be caught dead in such a skimpy thing anyway."

She handed me a grape-colored satin shirt. The front was covered in sequins, and the word Nashville was written across the back in big flowing white letters. Opal hooted. "That is one ugly shirt. What on earth was Mama thinking?"

I shrugged. Nothing Mama had done lately made any sense.

"You can wear it for Halloween," Opal said. "It's that scary."

My stomach was hurting, but it was the good kind of hurt, because I was so excited. The shirt made Mama's dream seem more real, as if it might come true after all, and she would come back for us like she promised. I held the shirt to my face, trying to breathe in the Mama-smells I remembered. I imagined her fingers grasping the pencil as she scribbled the note. I imagined her taking the envelope to the post office, licking the stamps, watching the package disappear down the mail chute.

"Come on," Opal said, and we took our presents and the rest of the mail to the house.

When Aunt Julia saw the bikini and the shirt, she shook her head. "You need winter coats, and Melanie sends a swimsuit. I don't know why I should be surprised."

After supper we listened to the last game of the

World Series on the radio, even though Opal wanted to listen to the Top Forty DJ from Oklahoma City. Aunt Julia picked up Mozart and sat forward in her chair, her head cocked toward the radio. When the Pirates scored their first run, she yelled so loud Mozart shot off her lap and hid behind the curtains. I cheered just like I was in the stadium watching the game in person. Opal rolled her eyes and turned the pages of her magazine louder than was necessary, to remind us of how much she was suffering.

"Bottom of the ninth," the announcer said. "The Yankees and Pirates are tied, nine all, Mazeroski at the plate. The count is one ball, no strikes. Here's the windup . . . and the pitch. A fastball to the inside . . ." There was a loud crack on the radio, then the announcer yelled, "Mazeroski has a hit! It's going, going . . . it's a home run! The Pirates have won the championship! What a finish to this World Series!"

"Way to go, Pirates!" Aunt Julia's face was pink, and for once she was actually laughing. "What a great game."

"I thought you were a Dodgers fan," I told her, when the announcer signed off.

She scratched Mozart's ears. "I care more about the game itself than the individual teams. You can't live in Oklahoma and not like baseball. Mickey Mantle is originally from Spavinaw, you know."

I nodded. I'd read about how the Mick had played

baseball in homemade uniforms when he was in high school in White Bird, and then gone on to be one of the best players in the world. He'd just finished eight straight years of batting in more than a hundred runs each season. Back home me and Daddy listened to the Yankees games every chance we got. "Boy, I wish I'd been in Tiger Stadium last month when Mickey hit that six-hundred-foot homer," I said.

"Six hundred and forty-three feet, to be exact," Aunt Julia said.

I guess my mouth must have dropped open, because then Aunt Julia said, "Well, don't look so surprised. My daddy taught me to love baseball when I was about your age. He took me to a game once, up in Oklahoma City, just the two of us. It was one of the best days of my life."

Later I lay in the dark with my new shirt under my pillow, listening to the house sounds, trying to fall asleep. But Cooley's words from that afternoon kept bouncing around in my head. I went downstairs to the living room, switched on the light, and took Aunt Julia's dictionary off the shelf. Guess what? Cooley was right. Garnets are only semiprecious.

CHAPTER TEN

If I had been the boss of Willow Flats Junior High School, I'd have abolished it instantly. It was nothing like my school in Mirabeau, where I had Jean Ann to keep me company at lunch and where I knew most of the answers to the teachers' questions. School in Willow Flats was harder. Even though I paid attention, when Mr. Stanley called on me in math class, I always got the answer wrong.

History class was even worse. It was like Miss Browning had it in for me from the very beginning, and I didn't even know why. She was always picking on me by telling me to speak up, or taking points off my papers because I forgot to write in complete sentences. So unfair.

It wasn't even Halloween yet, and she had already sent

two notes to Aunt Julia about how I was not working to my full potential. I buckled down and memorized the Bill of Rights and the Preamble to the Constitution for the weekly quizzes, but mostly I stayed quiet, desperately trying to come up with an idea for my semester project.

Powla's art class was the only thing that made school bearable. I soaked up her words the way biscuits soak up gravy. I lived for third period, when she would bring out her slides and talk to us about making art as if we were professional artists.

On the day before Halloween she began with a picture by a painter named José Orozco. It showed a teacher wearing a blue dress and a sour expression that would stop a clock. Standing at her feet were a bunch of kids who all looked alike. Same clothes, same haircut, same grim expression. In the background was a gang of adults who also looked the same. The women wore shapeless white smocks; the men were dressed in identical gray suits and ties.

"This year we are exploring art as a way of telling stories about man and society," Powla began in her soft accent. "Who can tell us what Orozco is saying with this piece?"

Lee Crockett shifted his huge feet and said, "They want us all to be the same."

"Who is 'they'?" Miss Mendez asked.

Nathan Brown raised his hand. "The government? School officials, maybe? People in authority."

In the light of the projector bulb Nathan's face seemed more grown-up and serious. My stomach fluttered. He'd been sitting in that same chair all semester, but now it was like I was seeing him for the first time. I couldn't take my eyes off him.

Miss Mendez said, "Yes. Orozco is commenting on the effects of conformity."

I thought about the first day of school, when Mr. Conley had told me the train problem was meant to teach me to think, yet Miss Sparrow had spent half the period telling us how to write our headings the same, use the same color ink, fold our papers the same way. I remembered the day Miss Browning had told us about Socialists and Communists and about how a man named Karl Marx said all of history is really the story of struggles between the different classes in society. I thought about the Negroes at the Louisiana sit-ins, who were demanding their rights as citizens, the same as white people. It seemed the freedoms I'd memorized for my history quiz weren't really for everyone. Instead, they belonged to the most powerful people, who made up the rules everybody else had to follow.

An imaginary lightbulb went on above my head. The differences between what they teach you in school and what goes on in the real world seemed like an interesting topic for my history project. I took out a piece of paper and started sketching some ideas, my eyes jumping from my paper to Orozco's picture, then to the gorgeous Nathan Brown.

Even in art class, though, Mama's absence hung over me like a big cloud. In the middle of making potato prints or learning about Diego Rivera and how he got into major trouble for his paintings, I'd start wondering where Mama was and what she was doing in Music City, and whether she missed me and Opal at all. I felt like I was floating in space with nothing solid to hold on to.

Miss Mendez switched off the projector, turned the lights on, and announced that our class would paint the scenery for the all-school play in the spring. "We won't have time to do it during class," she said, "so those who are interested will have to stay after school."

Just my luck. Finally school offered something I really wanted, and I couldn't have it because I lived at the end of the known universe with an eccentric aunt who refused to drive a car. Powla went on talking about the project, but I scarcely heard a word she said. I slouched in my seat, my tamped-down anger so sharp I could almost smell it.

"Pssst! Garnet!" Cooley leaned across the aisle. "What are you wearing for Halloween tomorrow?"

"None of your beeswax."

The bell rang, ending the class. Five minutes later I was standing at my locker when Miss Mendez came up behind me. "I hope you'll help us paint the scenery."

She had to shout a little because the hall was full of noisy people going to lunch.

"I can't." I grabbed my greasy lunch sack out of my locker and slammed the door shut.

"Why not?"

"I ride the bus home. There's nobody to pick me up after school."

"I see." She chewed on her bottom lip. "I'm pretty sure Nathan Brown will be working with us. Perhaps his mother would give you a lift."

As bad as I wanted to paint the scenery, the last thing I wanted was for Nathan to find out where I lived. Except for the Barton house, Aunt Julia's was the worst in Willow Flats. Having Nathan see Aunt Julia's place would be too humiliating.

"I have to help my aunt after school." I hated lying to my favorite teacher when she had been so great to me. Even more, I hated feeling ashamed of the place I was forced to call home.

Miss Mendez put her hand on my shoulder. "It would be a valuable experience for you, Garnet. Talk to your aunt. See if you can work something out."

"Okay," I said, knowing I wouldn't. I took my sketchbook and my lunch upstairs and pushed through the double doors to the fire escape. From there I could see the river winding through the rust-colored trees and the brown grass of the pasture beside the road. I tried to make some sketches for my history project, but disappointment had killed my enthusiasm. I swallowed a few bites of greasy sausage and waited for the bell to ring.

I slogged through history, gym class, and Mr. Riley's fascinating lecture on the way colds are spread. As if we hadn't heard the same thing every year since kindergarten.

"Don't forget, people," he said as the last bell rang. "Your projects are due next Friday."

My report on the circulatory system, complete with a model of the heart made out of red and blue cellophane, was already done. One advantage to being unpopular: There's always plenty of time for homework.

Seth wasn't on the bus that afternoon, and neither were the Judd boys, so Opal sat with me. When Sunday let us off at the mailbox, we saw a black car in the yard, and a hundred different things popped into my head. I thought it was probably someone visiting from Aunt Julia's church, but I hoped Mr. Hancock had come in person to deliver Daddy's disability money or, even better, that Mama had got her record contract after all and had come to take us to Nashville in style.

The door opened just as we reached the porch, and a man came out carrying a stack of papers. He jammed his hat onto his head, got into his car without saying boo to us, and drove off. We went in.

"Who was that?" Opal dropped her books onto the sofa.

"He works for the county welfare office," Aunt Julia said wearily. We followed her and Mozart to the kitchen.

"Welfare?" Opal echoed. "Are we that broke?"

"Just about." Aunt Julia took the last three potatoes from the bin and picked up her paring knife. "I don't understand it. Your daddy's checks were due weeks ago."

"So we're going to get potted meat and powdered milk from the government, just like the Bartons," I said.

"For a little while." Aunt Julia dropped the potatoes into the pot. "There's no shame in being poor." But shame and anger at Mama crashed around inside my head, and there was nothing I could do about it.

While the potatoes boiled, we drank tea and listened to the news on the radio. President Eisenhower talked about why the United States had gotten involved in Laos and Cuba. Senator Kennedy said America had lost friends around the world, thanks to the Republicans, and that he would be changing things big-time if he were elected president. The newsman said some people were afraid to vote for Mr. Kennedy because he was a Catholic and might start taking his orders from the Pope. Senator Kennedy said he would quit before he'd let that happen.

Then a song came on, about a girl who was afraid to come out of the water because she was wearing a tiny yellow bikini.

"Listen, y'all!" Opal said. "They're singing about that silly swimsuit Mama sent!"

Aunt Julia laughed, a booming sound so unexpected I temporarily forgot that I was mad at the whole world. I laughed too, until my eyes watered. When the song ended, Aunt Julia wiped her eyes with the corner of her apron and said, "Garnet, what are you wearing tomorrow for Halloween?"

"I'm not wearing a costume."

"Well, of course you are. Opal is wearing one, aren't you, Opal?"

"Not really. In high school it's different."

"Oh." Aunt Julia spooned potatoes and fatback onto our plates. "We must figure out something for Garnet, though. It's important to fit in at school."

She set her jaw, and I could see it was no use trying to talk her out of it. Once Aunt Julia made up her mind about something, she was as persuasive as a rock in a sock.

"I told her she should wear that awful shirt Mama sent," Opal said, stirring more sugar into her iced tea. "Honestly, have you ever seen anything so hideous?"

"That's not a bad idea," Aunt Julia mused. "You could dress up like a country singer, Garnet. I'll lend you my hoop earrings and a scarf. Patsy Cline always wears a scarf."

Maybe I should have seen disaster coming, but I was

tired of being an outsider. For just one day I wanted to feel like I belonged, even if it meant dressing up like a fool. I grabbed on to Aunt Julia's idea like a drowning person to a rope, and the next morning I set off for the bus wearing my black skirt, Aunt Julia's scarf and earrings, and my purple shirt.

"Well, look at you!" Sunday Larson said when she opened the bus door for me. "Don't you take the rag right off the bush! Where'd you get that shirt?"

"My mother sent it from Nashville."

"Turn around, let me see the back."

The bus idled in the road while Sunday admired my costume. Opal flopped down on a seat at the back of the bus with Cheryl and pretended she'd never seen me before in her life. Sunday finished admiring my shirt, and we took off.

When we stopped at the Bartons' place, two of the girls got on and took a seat across the aisle from me. Darlene, the one who sat behind me in homeroom, wasn't there. The oldest one, Polly, was in high school like Opal, so she wore her regular clothes, a man's plaid shirt over a brown print dress. The younger one wore faded black tights and a bumblebee body cut from paper sacks and colored with crayons. She leaned across the aisle and said, "Your shirt is pretty."

"Thanks. Your bee costume is pretty too."

"No, it isn't. It's dumb. I wanted a princess costume with a real tiara, but my mama said we couldn't afford—"

"Hush, Annalee," Polly hissed. "Stop telling people our business."

Near the end of our route, with the bus almost full, we rounded the curve down by Aunt Julia's church, and the Underwood girls, who usually rode with their daddy to school, were standing in the road waving us down.

Sunday stopped the bus and hollered out the window, "Need a ride, girls?"

"Yes, ma'am," Faith said. "My daddy left early this morning to preach a funeral in Lawton. A good friend of his went fishing, stood up in his boat to reel in a bass, and just keeled over dead. My daddy says that proves people need to be ready for Heaven whenever God decides he's ready for you."

Sunday cranked open the door and the girls climbed on. "That's more sermon than I needed at this hour," Sunday said. "But I will allow, Miss Faith, you got your daddy's silver tongue."

Faith and Hope sat down behind me. Since her mission of mercy had ended on the first day of school, Faith had kept her distance from me, but this morning she leaned forward as we started on down the road. "That's some shirt, Garnet."

Hope nodded. "Who are you supposed to be? The purple people eater?"

Annalee Barton turned around in her seat and said to Faith, "How come you ain't wearing a costume? Don't you know it's Halloween?"

"We don't believe in Halloween," said Hope. "Halloween is for heathens."

"What's a heathen?" asked Annalee.

"Never mind," Hope said.

But Faith couldn't resist the opportunity to preach to a captive congregation.

"A heathen," she announced, "is a person who isn't religious. Heathens dress up like ghosts and ghouls and poke fun at death because they're scared of where they're going when they die. But once you're baptized, you become a whole new person inside and you aren't afraid of the fires of hell anymore."

Annalee jumped into my lap and burst into tears. "I don't want to die in a fire!"

"Now look what you've done!" I glared at Faith.

Sunday said, "Faith, honey, maybe you'd better save your sermons for church."

"Jesus preached to everyone, whenever he had the chance." Faith checked to make sure Sunday wasn't watching, then stuck her tongue out at me.

That was the last straw. I nudged Annalee off my lap and whipped around in my seat. "You aren't Jesus!" I told Faith. "And you're scaring the daylights out of a little kid."

"Mind your own business, heathen."

"What did you call me?" I was on my feet, leaning over Faith's seat, trying to keep my balance as the bus swayed around a curve and headed up the long driveway to the schoolhouse.

Sunday pulled into the parking area and killed the engine. Inside the bus a strange kind of excitement was building, the kind that comes just before a fight breaks out, when everything stops and everybody waits to see who will throw the first punch. But then Sunday cranked open the door and hollered, "Everybody out!"

She got out first and stood by the steps as the bus emptied. When I reached the bottom step, she pulled me aside. "I appreciate that you were defending Annalee, but it won't do any good to argue religion with people. Especially with preachers' kids." She jerked her thumb toward the schoolhouse. "Go on now, and watch that mouth of yours."

I headed inside to my locker and nearly collided with Cooley. He was dressed all in black, a red cape over his shoulders. He was wearing long fake teeth and had drawn a bolt across his neck with a black eyebrow pencil. Obviously he couldn't decide whether he wanted to be Frankenstein's monster or a bloodthirsty vampire. "Hey," he cackled. "What's buzzin', cuzzin?"

"I'm not your cousin." I was still mad at him for pointing out the truth about garnets, but he looked so ridiculous I couldn't help smiling.

"Eureka!" he shouted to Nathan Brown, who was

looking cuter than ever in an old-fashioned baseball uniform stuffed with padding. "The precious gem smiles at last!" Then he fell all over himself laughing. Nathan shook his head and grinned at me and the bottom dropped out of my stomach. Before I could work up the nerve to say something brilliant, the bell rang and we headed to English class, where all the trouble started.

First off, everybody except Faith Underwood was dressed as a character from literature or history. A couple of boys were dressed as Abe Lincoln. One was dressed all in white, like Mark Twain. Cindy Lawless, who sat two seats behind me, wore a spider costume with the words "Some Pig" pinned to it. Then Starch and Vinegar decided it would be a good idea for everybody to model their costumes, like show-and-tell from when we were in kindergarten. It was a dumb idea, but she wouldn't change her mind.

Cooley volunteered to go first. He gave an exciting summary of Mary Shelley's book about Frankenstein, acting out the part of the German student who figures out how to infuse life into ordinary matter, only to be destroyed by his own creation. He said *Frankenstein* was one of the most interesting books he'd ever read.

"If you're supposed to be Frankenstein's monster, then what's with the vampire teeth?" Cindy asked, smoothing her spider costume. "The monster wasn't a vampire, too, was he?"

"No," Cooley said. "but after I finished reading *Frankenstein,* I read *Dracula* by Bram Stoker, and I realized both the stories are about how man struggles against the evil impulses hidden deep down inside everybody, no matter how good they try to be."

I just stared at him, dumbstruck. It was hard to believe that behind the constant teasing and all-around goofiness, there was an intelligent boy who thought deeply about things.

Miss Sparrow seemed surprised too. She smiled and nodded to Cooley and made a mark in her grade book. I figured that Cooley had just aced his English grade for the whole semester.

Cooley took his seat, looking way too pleased with himself, and then Nathan stood up, modeled his baseball uniform, and said Babe Ruth was the greatest baseball player in the universe, and that he, Nathan, had a genuine autographed Babe Ruth baseball that his grandfather had given him. "But my mother wouldn't let me bring it to school. It's too valuable to risk losing it."

"Thank you, Nathan," Miss Sparrow said. "Who'll be next?"

Margie Carter, dressed in long earrings and a gold taffeta prom dress at least three sizes too big for her, gave a ten-minute lecture on Cleopatra. "She's my hero because she didn't let guys push her around."

She rustled back to her seat. Miss Sparrow's gaze

swept over the room. I kept my head down, hoping she'd forget about me, the stupid new kid who got everything all wrong. So of course she said, "Garnet? Your costume looks interesting. Come on up here and tell us about it."

A sound like a swarm of mad bees started inside my head. I tried to think of somebody important who had run around in oversize earrings and a tacky sequined shirt, but my mind was a blank. "I didn't know we were supposed to dress up as a character," I muttered.

"What?" Miss Sparrow said. "Speak up, please."

"I didn't know!" I yelled. "I'm not dressed up as anybody! My mother sent me this stupid shirt."

I pushed open the door and ran down the hall.

"Garnet!" Miss Sparrow called me back, but I turned left at the end of the hall and ran to my locker. Right there in the middle of the deserted hallway, I stripped off the purple shirt and pulled on the sweat-stained T-shirt I'd worn for our physical fitness test the week before. I wadded up the purple shirt and went out the back door to the garbage cans behind the cafeteria. I stuffed it into the garbage and watched it disappear under a blob of green beans, congealed gravy, and sour milk. Then I headed home.

I cut across the school yard and started up the road. A cold wind whipped through the trees and dried the tears on my face. How had my once-normal life turned into such a train wreck? Why couldn't I do anything right?

A car came up the road behind me, and I ducked into the trees. The car slowed as it made the curve, then stopped. Charlie Twelvetrees got out and stood in the road, his head cocked to one side, listening. Ordinarily I'd have been happy to see him, because he told the most interesting stories of anybody I knew, but right then I didn't want to talk to anyone. I squatted behind a thick stand of bushes just beginning to shed their leaves.

"Garnet Hubbard," Charlie said into the quiet. Like he could see right through the thicket to my hiding place. He crossed the road and started toward me like a hunter tracking game.

I stepped out of the shadows. "Hey, Charlie."

"You're not in school."

"I quit." I shivered in my thin shirt.

"What happened?" Charlie took off his sweater and handed it to me. I burrowed into it, into the river smells and the smells of wood shavings and smoke. We sat on the brown stubbled grass and I told him everything. About going on welfare, about losing my chance to work on the scenery for the play, and about how everybody hated me because I was stupid and a heathen to boot.

"Too many problems for one girl." Charlie rose in a graceful motion that made him seem a whole lot younger than Sunday said he was. "Wait here."

The wind stirred the red dust on the road. A flock

of blackbirds circled overhead with a quiet, shimmering sound. Charlie opened the trunk of his car, took out a leather pouch, and came back to where I sat. He squatted in front of me and dumped three tiny carved wooden dolls and a hollowed-out wooden egg into my hand.

"Worry dolls," he said. "They're magic."

Okay, I was twelve years old and I'd been around the block a few times. I didn't believe in magic any more than I believed in Santa Claus or Charlie's wooden bird carving, or Mama's Madame Fortuna card game. But I wanted to. "How do they work?"

"At night before you sleep, think of your three biggest worries. Tell one worry to each of the dolls and put them under your pillow. While you dream your spirit dreams, the dolls will try to solve your problems."

"Spirit dreams?"

Charlie nodded. "There are ordinary dreams, like dreaming you're riding a roller coaster or taking a trip somewhere. And there are spirit dreams that reveal the longings of our souls. In spirit dreams our problems are solved."

It made me want to cry the way Charlie trusted that a total disaster could somehow work out okay if you only believed. A raven fluttered in and settled on a branch just above our heads. Charlie studied it for a long time.

"A good sign," he said at last.

I got up and dusted off my skirt. "I'd better go home before somebody from school tells Aunt Julia I'm missing."

"You wouldn't want to worry her," Charlie agreed, getting to his feet. "Come on. I'll give you a ride."

When we got to Aunt Julia's, she was standing in the yard with Sunday Larson. Me and Charlie got out of the car.

"There you are, Patsy Cline!" Sunday said. "Where's that pretty purple shirt of yours?"

Before I could answer, Aunt Julia said to me, "Ida Wink called the store and said you'd run off. What in the world made you do a thing like that?"

"I don't want to talk about it." I gave Charlie his sweater back.

He folded it and said to Aunt Julia, "Garnet Hubbard has many worries. A day away from school will be good medicine."

Aunt Julia sighed. "What am I going to do with you, Garnet?"

"I'll call the school and let them know she's safe," Sunday said. She jumped into her truck and roared off.

Charlie said to Aunt Julia, "Election Day's coming up on Tuesday. Will you need a ride to the polls?"

"I'd be obliged to you, Charlie."

"It's no trouble. I'll be by around ten." Charlie looked down at me. "When you're young, life seems long, but when you're as old as I am, you'll realize it's all too brief. Don't waste it yearning for what you can't have."

"Thank you for the worry dolls," I said.

Charlie's eyes were suddenly so watery I thought he was crying. But I don't know. Maybe it was allergies.

CHAPTER ELEVEN

When I went back to class the following Monday, nobody, not even Cooley, said a word about what had happened. Now that my anger had cooled, I was sorry I'd thrown away my only present from Mama, but there is no use crying over spilled milk.

Miss Sparrow handed out new reading assignments and gave a pop quiz on conjunctions and prepositions. Cooley complained that it was no fair giving a test right after a major holiday, especially since we were still keyed up from a whole weekend of eating too much candy. Faith piped up and said Halloween was not a real holiday. Old Starch and Vinegar shushed them both with the threat of more homework, and after that the room went quiet until the bell rang and we were dismissed.

"Garnet?" Miss Sparrow said as everybody headed out the door. "Will you wait a moment, please?"

"Uh-oh," Cooley said, pushing his Coke-bottle glasses back onto his nose. "You're in trouble now."

"Shut up."

"You shut up."

Miss Sparrow said, "Go along, Cooley. I can do without any more comments from you today."

When the room was empty, Miss Sparrow shoved her hands into the pockets of her sweater and perched on the edge of her desk. "I owe you an apology."

"Ma'am?"

"I should have told you to come dressed as a character from literature or history. It's been our seventh-grade tradition for almost forty years, and everyone looks forward to it. I forgot you're new here and wouldn't know."

"You shouldn't have called on me to talk about my costume."

"Right," Miss Sparrow said. "I didn't intend to embarrass you, but I did, and I am truly sorry."

I was still mad, but what can you say when an adult apologizes to you? Especially if that adult is an English teacher armed with a red marking pen and a grade book. "It's okay."

She smiled. "Good. I'm glad we've put this behind us." She scribbled a late pass for me, all business again. "See you tomorrow. Don't forget your homework."

. . .

Election Day came and Senator Kennedy barely beat
Mr. Nixon for the job of president of the USA. Then,
as if we didn't already have enough to do getting our
history projects done, Miss Browning assigned a
research report about our new president. On Saturday
I begged a ride to the library with Sunday Larson, hoping that this time she'd steer clear of the chicken sale.

The library occupied a dingy room in the basement
of the Willow County Courthouse. Metal shelves full of
dog-eared novels, a few biographies, and a bunch of
theology books lined the walls. In the corner sat a
wooden table with people's initials carved into the top,
and a couple of chairs. The librarian turned out to be
Celestial's mother.

"You must be the Hubbard girl," she said, when I
asked her if she had any books about Mr. Kennedy
suitable for a seventh-grade history report.

"Yes, ma'am."

"Well, I hope you like school here," Mrs. Jones
said, getting up from behind her desk. "Celestial just
loves it."

She pointed to a desk covered with newspapers
from Oklahoma City and Dallas and New York City,
all filled with stories about the election and pictures of
our new president.

"We don't have any books yet," Mrs. Jones said,
"but these papers should give you all you need for your

report." She glanced at her watch. "I work half days on Saturdays, so I'm afraid I must go, but feel free to stay as long as you want. If you decide to check out books, just fill out the cards and leave them in that box over there. We operate on the honor system when no one is around."

I pored over the newspapers and copied down some facts about Mr. Kennedy: that he saved his Navy crewmates when his PT boat was destroyed, and he wrote a bestselling book about courage that won an important prize. That he had a wife who liked to ride horses, and he had one kid and another one due any minute. When I figured I had enough facts to satisfy Miss Browning, I poked around the library. I checked out a couple of Nancy Drew mysteries, then walked over to the drugstore to meet Sunday.

She was sitting in the truck reading a romance comic book. I opened the truck door, relieved to see that the cab was still a chicken-free zone. Sunday marked her place with her finger. "All finished?"

"Yes, ma'am."

"Hungry?"

"A little."

"Let's grab some burgers."

I dumped my stuff in the cab and followed Sunday into the drugstore, feeling a little guilty about going for a burger when Opal was home having sausage and biscuits again, but not guilty enough to turn down the invitation. Me and Sunday ordered burgers, fries, and chocolate sodas. We sat in a red leather booth and listened to the jukebox. When the food came, I felt like a piece of heaven had floated into the Rexall. The meat was sizzling and smothered in cheese. The pickles were cold and crunchy, just the way I like them. When I had all but licked the plate clean, Sunday paid the check and we went home to find Aunt Julia standing on the porch with her pocketbook over her arm.

"I'm sorry to bother you, Sunday," she said as I opened the truck door and stepped out, "but I wonder if I could have a ride to Herman's store."

My stomach jumped. Daddy's check must have arrived, and my warm winter coat could be ransomed at last from the department store's layaway.

"It's no trouble," Sunday said. "Hop in."

"Stay here with Opal," Aunt Julia said to me. "I'll be back in an hour and we'll make supper."

I went inside. It took me a minute to realize that Aunt Julia's piano was gone.

"She sold it," Opal said from the couch. "The preacher's wife bought it for choir rehearsals. Mr. Underwood brought his truck for it just after you left this morning."

"But Aunt Julia loved that piano! It belonged to our grandmother."

Opal shrugged. "It looks like we'll never see a

penny of Daddy's money. She had to do something to keep us from starving."

Finding out Daddy's check hadn't come after all was a letdown that left me feeling mad at my mother all over again and feeling like one huge burden to Aunt Julia. I went upstairs and started working on my President Kennedy report, but I soon got bored with it and opened one of my Nancy Drew mysteries. Normally I loved reading about Nancy's adventures, but now I was too upset to concentrate. I tossed the book onto the bed and took my worry dolls from their hiding place in my underwear drawer. Even though it wasn't yet time for dreaming a spirit dream, and even though I had plenty of doubts about whether the dolls would really work, I didn't think it would hurt to give them a try. So I gave them each a problem to solve. Number one: Find Daddy's disability money and make him get well superfast. Number two: Make me special, like Opal. Number three: Knock some sense into Mama so she'll come back.

Pretty soon Sunday came back with Aunt Julia, and me and Opal helped her carry in shopping bags, shoe boxes, and half a dozen sacks from Sunday's grocery store. It felt almost like Christmas. Besides our coats, Opal and I each got a pair of boots, two pairs of socks, and flannel pajamas. I was thrilled with the pj's, since nights in Aunt Julia's drafty old house were already getting cold, and it wasn't even truly winter yet. But

Opal held hers out like she thought they'd give her cooties and said, "These will make me look like I'm fifty years old."

"Beggars can't be choosers," Aunt Julia snapped.

"I'm sorry you had to sell the piano," I said.

"No sense in talking about that." Aunt Julia turned on her heel and stalked to the kitchen to make supper.

She fried some ham and opened cans of sweet potatoes and corn. After weeks and weeks of eating nothing but sausage and biscuits, the corn and potatoes tasted like a king's feast, even though back home in Mirabeau I never touched sweet potatoes. The food seemed to improve Aunt Julia's mood. While cleaned up the kitchen, she hummed along with the radio, which I had tuned to WSM in Nashville. It was almost time for the weekly broadcast of the Grand Ole Opry, and I didn't want to miss a single minute of it, in case they said Mama's name on the radio.

After we listened to songs by Little Jimmy Dickens, Roy Acuff, and the Carter Family, Aunt Julia fished a pencil from her apron pocket and started writing on the back of an envelope. She looked at me over the top of her glasses. "I'm making plans for Thanksgiving. Is there someone from school you'd like to invite?"

"Lord, no," I said. "I want to invite Charlie Twelvetrees."

Aunt Julia nodded. "That goes without saying. What about you, Opal? Would you like to invite Seth?"

"I don't like him anymore," Opal said. "Every time I turn my back, he's making goo-goo eyes at Cheryl. Being his girlfriend is too much work." She sighed. "I sure miss Waymon."

"I see," Aunt Julia said. "No Seth, then."

Opal said, "Besides, Travis invited me to spend Thanksgiving at his house."

"Travis Judd? Absolutely not!"

"Why not?" Opal's voice wobbled. "He's cute. He's fun to be with. All the kids at school like him."

"He's too old for you, for one thing."

"He's barely eighteen!"

"And you're fourteen."

"In three months I'll be fifteen."

Aunt Julia took off her glasses and pinched the bridge of her nose. "Opal, age is not the only issue. I've told you before, Travis comes from a tough family. You don't know what you'd be walking into."

"That's not his fault!"

"Maybe not, but I won't let you get mixed up with him. This discussion is closed." Aunt Julia put her glasses back on, picked up her pencil, and went back to her list.

"I hate you!" Opal yelled. "I hate this stupid, ugly house! I hate sausage and biscuits! I hate having no phone."

Aunt Julia looked up from her list and said quietly, "Well, Opal, there's the door."

Opal flew out of the house. The door banged shut behind her. I started to go after her, but Aunt Julia said, "Leave her alone. She'll calm down." She tapped her pencil against her teeth and went on as if nothing had happened, "We'll invite Sunday Larson, too. It just wouldn't be Thanksgiving without her green bean casserole."

And that was how me and Opal and Aunt Julia came to share our Thanksgiving Day turkey with Charlie and Sunday. Charlie brought a coconut cake from the bakery in town, and Sunday brought her casserole with French-fried onions on top. We had cornbread dressing and store-bought cranberry sauce, and a pumpkin pie with real whipped cream. It all tasted mighty fine, until Aunt Julia said that because of his bandages Daddy would have to sip his Thanksgiving dinner through a straw. Then I imagined him all alone in the hospital, in pain and missing Mama, and the pie stuck in my throat.

I wondered whether Mama was having turkey and pie at the ladies' hotel, whether she was remembering other Thanksgivings when we were still a family. Sorrow for everything I had lost came and sat on my chest, but I acted like I was having the time of my life so I wouldn't have to think about the fact that this year sitting around the table was an old maid, two lost girls, an ancient Indian, and an eccentric widow, all pretending we belonged together. Still, I was thankful

Charlie and Sunday were there, because I needed a family of some kind, even if it was a hodgepodge of people trying their best to make up for the pieces of my real family that were missing.

Charlie and Sunday helped us clear the table, and later we had slabs of Charlie's cake and mugs of hot coffee in the living room. Charlie told stories about the old days in Oklahoma when he had been a cowboy, herding cattle, branding calves, and weaving leather lariats. He talked about how the government broke its promises to the Cherokees and how his grandfather made the horrifying march called the Trail of Tears.

"No more sad tales, Charlie," Sunday said. She had brought her mandolin, and after that we sat around the fireplace singing songs we'd learned from the radio. When we sang about the Lord having the whole world in his hands, I heard a beauty in Aunt Julia's voice I hadn't noticed before. Hers was a voice full of the rain-washed warmth of a summer afternoon, and the cool crispness of a fall morning when the leaves begin to turn. It was a painting made of bright yellow, warm red, and silvery blue. A voice as good as anybody's you heard on the radio.

When we ran out of songs, Sunday and Charlie got up and said their good-byes. Sunday hugged Aunt Julia, then me and Opal. Charlie just nodded in that quiet way of his and picked up his hat.

We all went out to the porch. I stood between Opal

and Aunt Julia, feeling the cold November air around me. Charlie got into his car, and Sunday climbed into her pickup. "See you on the bus, girls!" she called. "Enjoy your weekend."

Charlie's headlights came on, shining like cat's eyes in the dark. He tooted the horn as he circled back toward the road, and we waved even though he couldn't really see us. Aunt Julia sniffed the air. "Smells like snow."

I remembered the one time an honest-to-Pete snow had come to Mirabeau. School was closed, and Mama and Opal and I went outside to make snow angels. Later we made ice cream out of snow, sugar, and vanilla. Daddy laid a fire in the fireplace and we roasted marshmallows, filling the whole house with the smell of warm sugar.

The memory burned my insides like I'd swallowed something too hot. I felt grief coming back on me like a blinding fog. I ran inside and pounded up the stairs to my room, trying to think of something that would make the memories go away, but nothing I thought of could stop my tears, and I gave up.

The door opened and Opal came in. "What's the matter with you?"

Since her fight with Aunt Julia over Travis Judd she'd hardly spoken to me. Like the whole thing was my fault.

"I *hate* this place. I want to go home."

"People in hell want ice water." Opal dug through the drawer for a sweater.

"You don't love Mama at all!" I said. "Don't you miss her even a little bit?"

A shadow passed over my sister's face. "What good would it do? She's off *chasing her destiny*!" Opal grabbed a book from the stack on the floor. "I'm going downstairs to read by the fire. It's too cold up here."

Five minutes later Aunt Julia came in. "May I sit down?"

I shrugged. It was her house. She could do whatever she wanted.

She lowered herself onto Opal's bed and stuck one leg out in front of her. "Want to tell me what's wrong?"

"The same thing that's been wrong ever since Mama left."

Aunt Julia nodded. "Homesickness."

"The worst part is all the lies she told."

"Nobody tells the truth all the time," Aunt Julia said. "Sometimes it seems human beings are just one big conglomeration of lies, big and small."

"Like the one you told the preacher about how you couldn't sing, even though you sound as good as people on the radio."

"Maybe at one time I did. I took lessons when I was younger. I dreamed of studying opera, but it didn't work out."

The idea of Aunt Julia warbling in Italian was such a shock to my brain that I almost forgot my misery. "What happened?"

"Melanie came along. By the time she was ten years old, both our parents were dead and I had to look after her, look after this place. I didn't have the time or money to continue my lessons."

"I don't get it," I said. "You're the one with the best voice, but Mama's the one running all over Nashville trying to be a singer."

"I wanted to sing just for the pleasure of it," Aunt Julia said, "but being famous and having fancy things was important to Melanie from the time she was old enough to talk. I did my best for her, but Melanie was ashamed of me, ashamed of her home. She couldn't wait to get away."

I felt my face turning red.

Aunt Julia went on. "I'd hoped to study again once she was older, but then the accident happened during her junior year of high school and that was that."

"Mama was in an accident?"

"She wanted to go to a music club in Tulsa, but we couldn't afford it, so she talked one of her classmates, a boy from Summerville, into taking her. She didn't consider for one second that she'd be ruining her reputation by staying out with him all night."

That didn't surprise me in the least. Mama never considered the consequences of anything she wanted to do.

"I borrowed gas money from Charlie Twelvetrees and took off after her." Aunt Julia stopped to collect her thoughts. "The weather was cold and drizzly that night. About an hour outside of Tulsa I hit a patch of ice and wrecked the truck. My foot was crushed so bad the doctors thought they'd have to amputate. But I hung on and eventually it healed. Now I have to wear special shoes, but I get along all right."

Remembering how Opal and I had made fun of her ugly shoes made me feel awful. I said, "If Opal stole my dream and nearly got me killed, I'd never forgive her."

"Oh, I held on to my anger for a long time." Aunt Julia smoothed a loose thread on Opal's quilt. "Melanie and I hardly spoke for years, even after you girls came along."

That explained why Mama and Aunt Julia never visited each other and why there were no pictures of her in our house in Mirabeau. But it didn't explain how Aunt Julia could be so content living a whole different life from the one she'd imagined. "How could you let Mama take everything?" I asked.

"I suppose some folks are meant to stand still so those around them can move." Aunt Julia sighed. "Even when she was just a little bitty thing, your mama's star burned too bright for a place like Willow Flats. But I reckon I'm just a stander."

I remembered how casually Mama had dumped me and Opal, how unconcerned she seemed about Daddy. Mama wanted to be famous so bad it didn't matter who all she had to hurt in the process.

"Mama's selfish," I said, almost to myself.

"She can be kind when she wants to."

Downstairs the clock chimed eleven. "I don't know about you," Aunt Julia said, yawning, "but I ate too much turkey. I'm so sleepy I can't keep my eyes open another minute."

I was getting tired too, but worries rattled around in my head like marbles in a Mason jar. "What will happen to us if Daddy's disability money doesn't come?"

"You let me worry about that."

"But we're taking welfare food, and you sold your piano. What will you sell next? Mama should come back and take care of her own kids."

"People don't always do what they should." Aunt Julia went to the door. "Wash your face and try to sleep."

Opal came in, grabbed her nightshirt, and went down the hall to the bathroom. The old water pipes shrieked as she turned the shower on. I got into my pajamas, slid under the covers, and tried to sleep, but I kept thinking about how Mama had walked all over everyone in her life to get what she wanted. She'd said there was a price to be paid for dreams, but she had neglected to tell me who all would be paying it. I didn't want to think of her as a bad person, but I could feel my hopeful image of Mama slipping away, and that scared me more than anything. I thought if only I could talk to her face-to-face, she'd see it was time to give up chasing the impossible and come home to what was real and true.

I got up and crossed the room to the desk, where I'd left my worry dolls. As I reached for them, one slipped from my fingers and rolled across the geography book Opal had left lying open on the desk. The worry doll rolled clear across Oklahoma and on through Arkansas, it rolled past Memphis and landed smack-dab on the *N* in Nashville. It seemed like a sign I'd been waiting for without even knowing it. In the deepest part of my heart an idea bloomed, grew, and became a decision. Since Mama wouldn't come back of her own free will, there was nothing to do but go to Nashville and get her.

CHAPTER TWELVE

I knew where to go to catch a bus for Nashville; I'd seen buses coming and going from a redbrick building next to the Rexall, just down the road from the courthouse. All I needed was money for my ticket.

On the day after Thanksgiving I walked up the road to Sunday's store and went in. Sunday set down the feed sack she was carrying and dusted off her hands. "Don't you look pretty as a movie star in that new red coat! What can I do for you, Garnet?"

"I need a job."

"I see."

"I was hoping I could work for you, sweeping up and dusting shelves. I can help you fill orders, too."

Sunday reached under the counter for two pieces of bubble gum. She handed me one and opened the other one for herself. She read the comic that came wrapped around the gum, grinned, and passed it to me. "You saving these?"

"Not really."

"You ought to. Collect enough wrappers and you can send away for free stuff."

I put the wrappers in my pocket and chewed the gum. It was so sweet it made my teeth hurt.

Sunday blew a fat bubble and let it pop. "Julia told me about your daddy's money being delayed, and I wish I could help you out, but Polly Barton works for me between Thanksgiving and Christmas. Her mama is too sick to hold down a job. Polly's working for me is the only way they can afford toys for the little ones. They won't take charity."

I could see how the Bartons needed money to buy Annalee's presents. She was still a little kid. And Opal said there was a new baby at home too. I was disappointed that Sunday couldn't offer me any work, but I couldn't blame the Bartons for wanting to stand on their own feet. I had nearly stopped eating lunch at school, rather than let Faith and Celestial know I was having potted meat and government cheese every day of the week.

Sunday patted my shoulder. "Julia called that Hancock fellow again the other day. They'll sort it out eventually. You shouldn't worry about it. Julia knows I'll let her have whatever she needs on credit."

On credit. "Would you lend me some money, then? I'll pay you back as soon as I can."

"How?" Sunday poked the tip of her tongue out and blew another bubble.

"I could get Aunt Julia to show me how to carve whirligigs and sell them at the crafts fair next spring. Miss Sparrow says it's the biggest event of the whole year."

Sunday scratched her head. "I don't know that there's much of a market for whirligigs, but I reckon I could advance you a few bucks. How much do you need?"

"Twenty dollars." I named the first number that popped into my head, and immediately wished I'd had the gumption to find out ahead of time how much a bus ticket cost.

Sunday's gray eyebrows went up. "That's a lot of money for a twelve-year-old. What do you need it for, anyway?"

Before I could make up a reason, Sunday snapped her fingers and grinned. "Don't tell me. Christmas presents for Julia and your sister, right?"

"Right." It wasn't exactly a lie. Bringing Mama home would be the best present of all.

"Don't worry," Sunday said, taking a twenty out of the cash register. "Your secret is safe with me."

"Thank you!" I tucked the money in my pocket. "I'll pay you back, I promise!"

Sunday nodded. "Hang around if you want to. I've got to feed my chickens."

As soon as the door slammed behind her, I called the bus company and found out that a one-way ticket cost seventeen dollars and change, and that eastbound buses left on Tuesdays and Thursdays at ten thirty and noon.

I hung up, full of plans.

"You're still here," Sunday said, making me jump.

"I was just going." I'd chewed all the sugar out of my bubble gum and my jaw was starting to ache. I spit the gum into the trash can by the door. "Thanks for the loan."

"Don't waste it on trifles. Use it for something unforgettable."

I walked home in the cold November wind, trying to work out all the details of my plan. I was pretty sure Powla would let me take my sketchbook up to the study hall on the second floor during her class. Lately she had used the first few minutes of each class period to talk about Diego Rivera, then we used the rest of the period to work on our own art projects. Most people were making self-portraits, but me and Nathan, Lee Crockett, and a couple of others spent every spare minute working on pictures for our history projects. I liked working in the study hall. It was deserted during third period, so I could push several desks together to make a table for my mural. The light was good, and nobody bothered me.

I could wait there until the tardy bell cleared the hallways. Then it would be a cinch to slip through the double doors leading to the fire escape, and from there to the road.

I wouldn't take a lot of clothes; Mama would buy whatever I needed once I got to Nashville. It would be just like old times, going shopping with Mama and stopping off on the way home for a cherry Coke and a burger. Afterward we'd pack up the truck, head back to Oklahoma for Opal, then hightail it to Mirabeau and wait for Daddy to come home. So many plans made me feel all jazzed up, like I'd eaten a whole box of chocolate drops.

When I got home, Aunt Julia was taking bills and catalogs out of the mailbox. I watched her expression go from hopeful to desperate as she shuffled through the stack, looking for a check. "No money today," she said, "but here's a letter from the hospital."

I grabbed the envelope and tore it open. At the top of the letter was a note from a girl named Sherry, explaining that she was a candy striper at the hospital who had helped Daddy write down what he wanted to say. Aunt Julia said, "Let's find Opal."

We went inside. Opal was sitting on the floor with Mozart and her ever-present *A Thousand Hints for Teens*. She looked up and leaned back stiff-armed on her palms. "What's up?"

"We got a letter from Daddy!" I waved the envelope in the air.

"Let me see!"

"I had it first. I'll read it to you."

"I'm the oldest, I should read it."

Aunt Julia said, "Quiet, both of you. *I'll* read it."

I dropped onto the floor beside Opal. Mozart climbed into my lap and flicked his tail. Aunt Julia put her glasses on and began.

My dear daughters,

First off, the docs say I am going to be almost as good as new once the skin grafts heal. I won't lie to you, the grafts hurt like the dickens, and when I am well, there will be scars. I won't be the same good-looking son of a gun on the outside, but on the inside I will be just the same, loving you both more than I can say.

I'm sorry I didn't say good-bye after your mama's party. If I'd known what was waiting for me around the next corner, I would have taken the time to tell you that the problems between your mama and me are not your fault, so don't blame yourselves for the way things turned out. Who knows? Maybe your mama will surprise us all and turn into the star she's always dreamed of being. Miracles happen every day.

I'll write again soon. Now that I can receive mail, I hope you'll write to me, too. Daytime television is not worth spit.

Love, Daddy

I scratched Mozart's ears, thinking that with Daddy on the mend I had more reason than ever to go after Mama. After the big fight on her birthday that ended our normal lives, I understood that even if she came back, things wouldn't be perfect. But my daddy was a charmer. Once we were all under the same roof again, he'd find a way to win her back.

The rest of the Thanksgiving weekend passed quietly. After church on Sunday, Aunt Julia settled down by the fire with her knife and her whirligigs, and Opal went to Cheryl's house to watch TV. I wished I'd been invited. Back home we watched *Bonanza,* our favorite western, every Sunday night. Opal had a major crush on Little Joe Cartwright, who was cute and curly-haired, but hot tempered. He was always punching out the bad guys before his dad could step in and cool him off. Adam Cartwright was my favorite. He was just as cute as Little Joe but quieter and more thoughtful, like Nathan Brown. Ben, their dad, owned their ranch, the Ponderosa. He was smart but unlucky in the marriage department. All three of his wives were dead.

Anyway, since I was home, I packed for my trip. I gathered a sweater, clean underwear, a spare toothbrush, and a comb, along with Sunday's twenty-dollar bill and a handful of change I'd found under the sofa cushions. I copied Mama's address from Aunt Julia's address book, took Mama's graduation picture from its frame, and slipped it into the musty pages of a Sherlock

Holmes mystery I'd found in the closet. Then I stuffed everything into my book bag and waited for Tuesday.

Monday was a normal day. Miss Sparrow read a poem by W. B. Yeats and spent the rest of the class period explaining what it meant. In art class I made some studies for my history project. Powla patted my shoulder and said for the umpteenth time that I had a gift for painting, but since I couldn't work on the scenery for the play, it didn't feel like a gift at all.

Mr. Riley handed back our projects on "Your Changing Body." He gave me a B on my map of the circulatory system, but I didn't really care. All I could think about was getting on the bus for Nashville.

After supper that night, Opal went upstairs to do her homework, and I tried to calm my nerves by helping Aunt Julia fold the laundry. We listened to the radio for a while, then I went upstairs. Opal was burrowed into her covers, head and all, apparently dead to the world. I got into my pj's, brushed my teeth, then wrote a note to leave for her the next day.

I have not been kidnapped. I have taken a bus to Nashville to bring Mama back. Tell Aunt Julia not to worry.

XOX Garnet

I tucked the note away and got into bed, but I was too jumpy to sleep. I tossed and turned, counting the stars that looked in through the window and listening to the wind in the trees. Sometime way after midnight the door to my room squeaked open. I sat up in bed and fumbled for the lamp switch. "Aunt Julia? What's wrong?"

"Shhh! It's me."

"Opal?"

"Quiet! You'll wake the warden."

"I thought you were asleep."

Opal threw back her covers to reveal her blankets and pillows arranged to look like a sleeping person. "That's what you were supposed to think."

"Where have you been?"

"Out with Travis."

"Aunt Julia will *kill* you if she finds out! What were you thinking?"

Opal slid out of her shoes and plopped onto her bed. "Travis is the only thing that makes life worth living around here. He's so fine, Garnet. He could have any girl he wants, and he picked me."

"But sneaking out . . . What if you'd been in a wreck?"

"He's a good driver."

"What if Aunt Julia finds out?"

"That's a risk I have to take. Half the girls in school are in love with him and just dying to take my place. He'll drop me if he thinks I can't handle the situation." Opal grabbed my hand, all serious, and said, "Swear a sister oath you won't tell."

I swore not to tell, but I didn't like it that my sister was turning into a stranger who kept secrets.

At breakfast I couldn't look Opal in the eye. I wasn't about to rat her out, but I could see she was playing with fire and I was scared of what could happen. Plus, I was so nervous about my trip that I could hardly swallow my scrambled eggs. I felt like I had to pee every ten seconds. After my third trip to the bathroom, Aunt Julia felt my forehead. "Are you feverish, Garnet?"

"No, ma'am, I'm just fine, thank you."

She frowned. "You sure have been acting peculiar the last few days. I hope you aren't coming down with something."

Then I forced myself to eat, so she wouldn't think I was too sick to go to school. When it was time for the bus, I waited until Opal was ready and standing by the door with her stack of books, then I hurried back upstairs to leave my note inside her *Thousand Hints* magazine, where she'd be sure to see it. I picked up my book bag, and at the last minute, stuffed my worry dolls inside. The bus rumbled up the road and stopped at the mailbox. Sunday honked the horn.

"Bye!" I pulled on my coat as I ran for the bus. Aunt Julia stood on the porch with a puzzled look on her face. All my running back and forth, and my umpteen trips to the bathroom, had unnerved her. I felt guilty for tricking her, but I told myself that my trip to Nashville was for her good too. The sooner

Mama came back, the sooner Aunt Julia could stop selling off her treasures to keep Opal and me in shoes and loaf bread.

At school the morning dragged on, the way time always drags when you are waiting for something important to happen. But at last, third period came and I headed for art class. Powla was coming out of the supply closet with a stack of canvases.

"Oh, Garnet. Good. Give me a hand with these, will you?"

I took half her load and propped the door open with my foot so we could go into the art room. She flicked on the light and set the canvases on the floor. Out in the hall the noise was picking up as people changed classes, slammed lockers, and pounded up the stairs to avoid being late to class. Nathan Brown came into the art room and dumped his books on the floor.

"Miss Mendez?" I began.

"Yes?"

"I was wondering if I could have the whole period today to work on my mural. The deadline is coming up and I still have a lot to do."

"I suppose so, but be sure to get the class notes from someone. Semester tests are coming up." Miss Mendez got busy setting up her slide projector. "Perhaps Nathan will lend you his."

I was thrilled at the thought of borrowing anything

that was Nathan's, but I could see the hesitation in his eyes, so I said, "That's okay. I'll ask Polly."

And that's how easy it was. I waited upstairs, just like I'd planned, until the tardy bell rang. When the halls emptied, I retrieved my book bag from my locker and climbed down the fire escape and onto the road. I passed the spot where Charlie had first given me the worry dolls, ducked under a barbed-wire fence, and followed an old truck path that wound past Charlie's place. Through the bare trees I could see the roof of his cabin and a ribbon of gray smoke curling out the chimney.

I passed behind Sunday's store, Aunt Julia's church, and Harold's Texaco, where we'd first got the bad news about Daddy's accident. By the time I got to town I was sweating, and my new winter shoes were pinching my feet. I leaned against the courthouse wall next to the clock tower and stood first on one foot and then the other, catching my breath. The clock struck eleven, and soon after, the Southern Plains bus came down the road and stopped at the station. Two men got off. The driver turned on the flashing parking lights and disappeared into the Rexall.

I crossed the road and went inside the terminal.

The ticket lady put on her glasses and peered through the little caged window at me. "May I help you?"

"A one-way ticket to Nashville, please."

"Nashville, Tennessee?"

"Yes, ma'am. That's the one."

She frowned. "How old are you?"

Something told me if I said I was twelve, she'd call the cops or the child welfare people Aunt Julia talked about, so I said, "I'm fourteen."

"And I'm the Queen of Sheba. You aren't a runaway, are you?"

"No, ma'am. My mama lives in Nashville. She's expecting me."

"Uh-huh." She punched her adding machine. "That comes to seventeen twenty-five, including tax."

I gave her Sunday's twenty. She inspected it like she thought it might be fake, but finally she put it in the drawer and handed me the change and my ticket. "Don't lose your ticket," she said. "You'll have to show it to the driver when you change buses in Little Rock."

I sat down on a bench inside the terminal. It wasn't noon yet, but I was starving. I counted my money. Besides the $2.75 in change from the twenty, I had 69 cents and the usual sausage and biscuit sandwich Aunt Julia had packed for lunch. I decided to eat it then so it wouldn't stink up my book bag all the way to Tennessee. I bought a Coke from the machine in the hallway and opened my paper sack. A man in a cowboy hat and boots came in and sat down on the bench by the door. He waved his ticket to the Queen of Sheba, who nodded to him and went back to her magazine.

Pretty soon the bus driver came in, still wiping

hamburger grease from his hands with a paper napkin. He looked at me and the cowboy and said to the Queen, "Is this everybody?"

"Yep."

We boarded the bus. The cowboy showed the driver his ticket, then sat way in the back, took off his hat, and closed his eyes. I sat in the second row from the front, by the window. The door whooshed shut and we took off.

It seemed like the time went fast. We followed the main road out of Willow Flats, crossed the river, and soon there was the sign welcoming us to Arkansas. The tires hummed along the highway as we passed old houses, barns and cotton gins, feed stores, and pool halls. We bumped across some weedy train tracks and the cowboy woke up and went to the little bathroom at the very back of the bus. By then I needed to pee real bad, but I was too embarrassed to walk past his seat and have him know where I was going.

By the time we rolled into the bus station in Little Rock, a steady rain was falling and it was getting dark. My bladder was about to explode. I made a beeline for the ladies' room, used the bathroom, and washed my hands at the cracked sink. I went back to the waiting room. I was starving. I bought a tuna fish sandwich and another Coke from the vending machines and ate at a table by the window. I tried to get interested in the Sherlock Holmes book I'd brought, but it was too hard to concentrate. I was anxious about seeing Mama, and worried she'd be mad at me for showing up out of the blue. I felt guilty for worrying Aunt Julia, guilty for lying to Powla. It hurt to know that neither of them would ever completely trust me again.

Another bus pulled up, and a bunch of teenagers came in. The girls rushed for the bathroom. The boys, most of them wearing blue and gold Future Farmers of America jackets, crowded around the sandwich counter, laughing and shoving each other, just fooling around. Somebody fed the jukebox. It whirred and clicked and then Elvis was singing "Jailhouse Rock."

Some of the kids started dancing, and I remembered Mama be-bopping around the kitchen when that song came on, her ruffled apron flying up when she spun around, wailing along with Elvis and pretending to play the trombone. I took her picture out of my book, and memories exploded inside my head like fireworks, bright splashes of color on the dark canvas of my new life. I thought of the way her blue eyes crinkled at the corners when she laughed. I remembered the year she stayed up all night making my Sleeping Beauty costume for Halloween, the way her face looked so serene and shining when we sang "Silent Night" in church at Christmas. Despite all she had done to disappoint me, I couldn't wait to see her.

A man's voice came over the loudspeaker,

announcing my bus. I tucked the picture away and followed the rest of the passengers outside.

The Nashville bus was crowded with college kids
heading back to school after the Thanksgiving break,
with old people, musicians with their guitar cases, and
mothers with sleeping babies, but I managed to grab a
seat by the window. The driver turned off the inside
lights and switched the heater on, and we pulled out of
the station, the tires swishing on the wet pavement.
Inside the darkened bus it was warm and quiet. People
slept, or talked in low voices. I leaned my head against
the rain-spattered window and let myself dream. I
imagined driving around Nashville with Mama, seeing
all the sights, going out for burgers and fries, then
staying up late to watch TV. Maybe we'd see Cordell
Jackson sing at the Opry. And maybe Mama would forgive me for being born and messing up her dreams.

CHAPTER THIRTEEN

Here's an important travel tip: If you're in a big hurry to get someplace, don't take the bus. After the stop in Arkansas, I figured we'd be in Nashville in no time, but the bus stopped in Memphis to change drivers, and again in Jackson to drop off some packages, and it was nearly lunchtime the next day when we finally rolled into Music City. Inside the Nashville bus station I went to the ladies' room and used a bunch of paper towels to wash up. I brushed my teeth, combed my hair, and changed my underwear. Mama was a real stickler for cleanliness, and I didn't want to get on her bad side by showing up at her hotel looking like a hobo.

Hunger pains were shooting through my stomach, but I was down to my last dollar, which I'd need to take the city bus to Mama's hotel. I ignored the smells of frying burgers and fresh coffee coming from the food counter and took a city bus schedule from a rack by the window. I studied it for a while, but I couldn't make heads or tails of the blue, green, and red lines that coiled and meshed like spaghetti in a bowl, and I couldn't find Fremont Street, where Mama's hotel was.

A Southern Plains bus driver was drinking coffee at the counter. I slid onto the stool next to him. "Excuse me," I said. "Can you help me find Fremont Street?"

He set down his coffee cup and spun around on his stool. "Let's have a look."

I handed him the bus schedule. He flipped it over, and there, in tiny print, was a list of street names. I felt dumb as a box of salt.

"Fremont, Fremont," he muttered, running his finger down the list. "Here it is. B twenty-six."

He showed me how to match the grid to the color-coded bus routes. "You want the green route. Bus number eighty-eight. There's a bus stop about a block up this street, in front of Woolworth's. You can't miss it."

"Thanks." I folded the schedule, picked up my book bag, and headed out the door and into a cold drizzle that made me wish I'd had enough gumption to bring an umbrella. I jogged up the street to the bus stop, where a couple of people waited with umbrellas and packages. By the time the bus swayed up the street and shuddered to a stop, my toes felt like icicles.

I got on and dropped my forty cents into the coin box. All the seats were taken, so I stood in the aisle, smushed between a couple of kids dressed in jeans and leather jackets and a woman in a nurse's uniform. A buzzer sounded. The driver pulled over and the kids in jeans got off. An old man with watery eyes got on and stood so close to me I could smell stale tobacco and his hot, sour breath. He smiled at me, showing a row of corn kernel teeth, but it wasn't a friendly smile. It creeped me out.

The nurse moved over and stood between me and the old man. "Which is your stop, hon?" she asked me.

"I'm going to Fremont Street."

She glanced out the window. "The next street is Western Avenue. Get off there and walk down three blocks to Fremont. I'll babysit Romeo here." She pulled the cord to signal the driver and the bus ground to a stop. "Be careful," the nurse said. "This isn't the safest neighborhood in town."

The bus pulled away, belching fumes and smoke. I crossed the street and walked to Fremont, looking for number 26. In my imagination I'd pictured a street with pretty buildings and glittery stores filled with beautiful clothes and fine jewelry. I imagined the ladies' hotel as a place with wide marble staircases, a revolving door, and a bellman to help you carry your stuff.

The reality was something out of a horror movie.

Brown weeds poked through the cracks in the concrete steps leading to the door. Half the windows were broken out and boarded up. Pea green paint was peeling off the shutters. In the gutter was a pile of broken beer bottles, plastic bags, and cigarette wrappers. It was hard to imagine Mama, who was so particular about every little thing, setting foot inside such a dump.

I opened the door. The hall was dark, and it smelled like pee and fried onions.

"Wipe your feet!" bellowed an old woman from behind a counter.

I looked around to see who she was yelling at.

"Yes, you, missy!" she hollered at me. "I'm talking to you."

I scraped my shoes on the doormat and went into the lobby. The woman said, "We don't rent rooms to kids."

"I'm here to see my mother, Melanie Hubbard," I said. Then I remembered Mama's new stage name: "McClain."

Now that I was finally here and about to see Mama, my heart sped up, and my palms got sweaty. I wiped them on my jeans, dug my comb out of my backpack, and raked it through my damp hair.

"Melanie, the blond one who acts like she's Grace Kelly?" The old woman gave a short laugh that sent her into a coughing fit. When she got her breath back, she said, "She's a looker all right, but I can't say beans about her singing. My regular tenants complained so often about her loud practicing, it was a relief when she moved out."

The room started to spin. "Mama moved?" Hot tears sprang to my eyes. "I have to find her!"

"Calm down! She left a forwarding address so I could refund her deposit. I've got it around here somewhere."

The woman opened a metal box filled with yellow index cards and began sorting through them. I was so exhausted and hungry I started to shake. Black spots swam before my eyes. I felt weightless.

"Hey, what's the matter?" The woman's voice sounded far away. "Are you sick or something?"

The next thing I knew, I was lying on the floor and she was pressing a wet washrag to my forehead. "You're white as a sheet, girl. How long has it been since you ate anything?"

"Yesterday. At the bus station in Arkansas."

"Where'd you come from?"

"Oklahoma."

"Can you sit up?"

She took ahold of my shoulders and helped me up. "Sit here and catch your breath. I'll be back in a minute."

The ceiling creaked as somebody walked around upstairs. A door slammed. A radio came on. The phone behind the desk rang and rang. Then the woman came back with a plate of saltines and a glass of milk. "This ain't much, but it's better than nothing."

Who would have thought crackers and milk could taste so good? I devoured it all and wiped my mouth with my fingers.

"Better?" The woman looked down at me, and I realized she wasn't as old as I'd thought. She'd just lived a slipping-down kind of life. I wondered whether she'd once had dreams of her own. It made me sad to look at her.

"What's your name?" she asked.

"Garnet."

"I'm Tina. You want some more crackers?"

"No, I'm okay. Thanks, though. The milk was real good."

She handed me a card with an address on it. "Here you go. She's at the Cumberland Apartments on Fairview Drive. Moved there a month ago."

I unfolded my map, my mind whirling. I couldn't believe a mother would move and not tell her own kids where she'd gone. Tina said, "You can take bus eighty-eight to Sixth Street. Transfer to the red line there. Transfer again at River Road and that bus'll take you all the way out to Fairview."

My heart sank.

"What's the matter now?" Tina asked.

"I don't have enough money for all those transfers. I'll have to walk."

"In this neighborhood? Not a smart idea. Besides, Fairview Drive is clear across town. You'd never make it before dark." She handed me a crumpled bill from her pocket. "This should do it."

I was so relieved I nearly started crying. "I'll pay you back. I promise."

"Forget it," Tina said. "Consider it my good deed for the day."

"Thanks." I picked up my stuff and started toward the door.

"When you see your mama tell her Tina says hey."

Outside, the streets were slick and shiny with rain. I walked back to the bus stop to wait. The clock on the bank building across the street said 3:25, but the dark clouds and cold wind made it seem later. Already the street lights were coming on. It seemed that hours passed before Bus 88 arrived, and hours more before I boarded the bus for Fairview Drive. As it lumbered down the noisy, traffic-clogged street, I watched the night lights coming on in the office buildings, and Christmas decorations twinkling in the store windows. It was getting dark when the bus let me off in front of the Cumberland Apartments.

Everything was spick-and-span. All the paint looked brand-new. Even though it was November, pots of red geraniums flanked every apartment door. Outside the office, arrows pointed the way to a pool, a gym, and a clubhouse. I figured Mama must be doing pretty well in the singing game if she could afford to live in such a nice place.

In the office a woman wearing a blue suit and pearls looked up Mama's name in a book. "Here we are. Apartment twelve. It's to your left, across from the pool."

I found apartment twelve and stood there gulping air, scared to ring the bell, almost wishing I hadn't come. But it was too late to turn back. I pressed the button and heard a faint chime. The door opened, and there was Mama.

Chapter Fourteen

"Garnet?" Her voice was a coiled spring. She clutched at her pink bathrobe and blinked like she was seeing a ghost. "What in the world are you doing here? Where's Opal? And Julia?"

"I came by myself." My backpack was getting heavy. My fingers and feet were freezing in the cold rain. "Can I come in?"

"Oh! Of course, come in!" Mama held the door and I went inside, so happy to see her that I wanted to fall into her arms and cry for about a million years. But I could tell she was mad at me for showing up, so I just stood in the hallway, looking around. The living room was bare, but I could see a bed, a dresser, and a mirror in the bedroom down the hall. There was a teakettle on the stove in the kitchen, a bunch of flowers in a vase on the kitchen table, and in the corner, a stack of sheet music and Mama's guitar.

Mama tied the sash of her robe and yawned. "Sorry. I worked a double shift and I'm beat." I followed her to the kitchen. She filled the teakettle, lit the stove, and took a couple of mugs from the cupboard. "Now. What's this all about, Garnet? How did you get here? Does Julia know you're here?"

We sat at the table waiting for the water to boil, and I told her about Daddy's disability money being all tangled up in red tape and about Aunt Julia selling her piano just to feed Opal and me. I told her how much I hated taking welfare food, hated Willow Flats School, hated Faith Underwood and Celestial Jones and their prissy friends. I told her about Charlie Twelvetrees and the worry dolls, and how they gave me the idea to come and fetch her.

"You never meant to come back for us," I said. "You and Aunt Julia lied." Now that I was there and rehashing all the injustices I'd suffered since August, I was getting madder by the minute.

Mama took a sugar bowl out of the cabinet. "Maybe we should have told you the truth from the beginning, but we were trying not to hurt you." She sighed. "I'm sorry you're having such a hard time of it, but there's nothing I can do."

"Yes, there is!" I yelled. "You can come home and

take care of your kids the way you're supposed to. You can take care of Daddy when he gets out of the hospital. That's what mothers do, *Melanie,* they take care of their families!"

I hurled my tea mug across the room. It shattered on the floor. I sat there shaking, my feelings for Mama bouncing back and forth between love and hate. Mama and I stared at each other. The kettle shrieked.

She didn't say a word. She took the kettle off the stove, swept up the broken pieces, then went down the hall to her bedroom and closed the door. I heard the shower come on, and then the sound of drawers opening and closing. Half an hour later she came out in a cloud of White Shoulders, looking perfect, acting like nothing had happened. "Are you hungry, precious?"

"Garnets aren't precious. I looked it up."

"You're precious to me."

"You've got a funny way of showing it."

"You came all this way just to hurt my feelings?"

"I came to tell you it's time to give up, Mama. It's time to come home and act like a regular mother. We had a life back in Texas. Don't you miss it, even a little bit? Don't you miss me and Opal? Don't you miss Daddy?"

"Honestly?" Mama said. "I miss my precious gems, but I do not miss Mirabeau even a little bit. Sometimes I miss your daddy. But he was gone so much, I felt like a single parent half the time anyway."

"He had to work! It wasn't his fault."

"You're defending him now, but don't you remember how mad you got last spring when he missed your baseball game?"

"He said he was sorry."

"He's a good man," Mama allowed. "One of the best in the whole world. But he drives me crazy. As long as there's fried chicken on the table and his truck is running good, he's a happy man. He never figured out that I need more than that."

It came to me then that Mama had spent so much time running over other people's feelings like they weren't as important as her own, that she couldn't see that her dream had turned into a curse that was hurting her whole family.

She eyed my dirty backpack. "Any clean clothes in there?"

"Yes."

"Are you hungry?"

"Yes."

"Go get cleaned up. We'll let Julia know you're safe and get something to eat."

Don't get me wrong. I was still mad as a hornet, but I was starving, too, so I didn't give her any more back talk. I bathed, washed my hair, and changed into my clean sweater.

"You look nice, honey," Mama said when I came

out of the bathroom. Her eyes were begging me to forgive her, but I couldn't.

"Can we go now?" I fluffed my damp hair with my fingers and fussed with my bangs so I wouldn't have to look at her.

Mama picked up her purse and keys. We walked across the parking lot and climbed into the truck. It still had the faint Daddy-smell I remembered, a mixture of leather, hair tonic, and spearmint gum.

Mama's driving skills had not improved one iota. She gunned the engine, spinning the tires on the wet pavement. Then we shot out of the parking lot and sped past stores and office buildings, laundromats, and restaurants. We passed the Ernest Tubb Record Shop and a yellow house with white painted curlicues above the porch. Mama said, "There's the Hilltop Café, where Ruby Lee Sims was discovered. One day she was waiting tables and singing backup, the next she was cutting records for RCA."

We turned down a side street lined with record stores and T-shirt shops, and stopped at a steak place. Mama cut the engine. "I'm telling you, Garnet, Nashville is a town where your whole life can change in the blink of an eye. All it takes is being in the right place at the right time."

We went into the restaurant. A hostess in a black dress led us past a darkened stage to a booth in the back, and handed us menus. The waitress came over and plunked down two glasses of water and silverware rolled up in white napkins. She smiled automatically, then did a double take.

"Well, hey there, Melanie. What are you doing here?"

Before Mama could say anything, the waitress said, "Wait. Let me guess. You love it here so much you just can't stay away even on your night off."

Mama tossed her head and laughed her movie-star laugh, like she thought a talent scout might be hiding behind the fake palm tree in the corner, scoping her out. "My daughter just arrived in town and she's famished, aren't you, precious?"

I nodded and opened the menu. Mama took it away from me and said to the waitress, "Bring us two specials, medium well, baked potatoes, hold the butter and sour cream on mine. Coffee for me, and . . . Garnet? How about a Coke, honey?"

"Okay."

"Be right back." The waitress grinned at me. "Welcome to Nashville, hon."

When she left, Mama slid out of the booth. "I'm going to call Sunday Larson. I won't be long." She dug through her purse and handed me some change. "Go play the jukebox if you want."

But I stayed put. I sipped my water and watched Mama feeding quarters into the pay phone at the back of the restaurant. She was wearing tight jeans, a white shirt with silver buttons, and suede high-heeled boots the color of butterscotch pudding. She hadn't said a word about her recording contract, but I figured she must be making pots of money to afford such nice clothes plus the apartment on Fairview Drive.

She hurried back to the booth and scooted in, dropping her purse on the seat. "Sunday's going to drive down to Julia's and let her know you're okay. I'll bet Julia is worried sick. It was thoughtless of you to just up and take off like that."

"It runs in the family."

"Don't be a smart mouth. Julia probably hasn't slept a wink since you left."

"I left Opal a note. She knew I was coming after you."

"Well, I'm sorry you've made a fruitless trip."

The waitress brought our food and the check. "Here you go," she said. "My shift's over and I'm outta here. See you tomorrow, Mel."

I salted my potato and dug in. Butter oozed out, warm and fragrant.

Mama said, "Tell me more about school. Surely there's something you like."

The good food was putting me in a better mood, so I told Mama about Powla's art class and about the painting I was working on for my history project. "It's called *American Dreams*," I told her. "Miss Mendez says she can tell from my sketches it's full of irony."

"Irony?" Mama laughed. "I'm not sure I know what that word means." She took a bite of potato and sipped her coffee.

Then I told her about the scenery project and how Miss Mendez said it would be good for me. "But it's an after-school thing, and there's no way to get home once the bus runs."

"I am truly sorry about that, Garnet," Mama said. "I know how it feels when you're just bursting to express all the emotions inside you, and there's no way to let them out."

The wistful way she said it made me realize that something about Mama had been altered since leaving Mirabeau. She wasn't the bubbly, hopeful person I remembered. She seemed older somehow. Maybe deep down she regretted running away, but she'd have died before admitting it.

She went on. "I had the same problem when I was in school. Julia had a bad wreck and demolished our truck. For a long time she couldn't drive, and by the time she was better, she'd lost her nerve. I had to bum rides from my friends, which was a huge pain in the old patootie, believe you me."

I waited for Mama to confess what I already knew: that the accident had happened because Aunt Julia was driving too fast, trying to save Mama's reputation. But

Mama motioned to another waitress for a refill on her coffee and changed the subject.

"How's Charlie Twelvetrees these days? I swear, that man is older than dirt."

"He's okay. He came to Thanksgiving dinner at Aunt Julia's."

Mama grinned. "I'll bet he brought coconut cake."

I had a big bite of steak in my mouth, so I just nodded. Then Mama asked me if I wanted dessert, but I was too full of steak and potatoes. After that we ran out of things to say. Mama finished her coffee and paid the check, and we went back to her apartment.

Even though it was barely nine o'clock, I was craving sleep. Mama turned down the bed and tucked me in, like she used to when I was little. She changed into her nightgown, washed her face, and slid under the covers beside me, and for a moment I was five years old again, happy and safe.

"I have to get up at four in the morning," Mama said, just as I was drifting off, "but you go ahead and sleep as long as you want. There's cereal and milk for breakfast, and bologna for sandwiches in the fridge. Keep the door locked and don't open it for anybody. I'll be back around three o'clock."

"Yes, Mama."

"Okay, then. Good night."

That was the last I remember before I fell into a

dream. Daddy and I were playing baseball in the yard, laughing and yelling, and Mama and Opal were sitting on the porch sipping lemonade. I could feel Daddy's rough palms on my hands as he showed me how to swing the bat. I could smell the sharp, clean scent of his spearmint gum and the sweetness of Mama's perfume. It seemed so real that when I woke up to the sound of a hard rain and remembered where I was, the hurt came down on me like a rock. Before I knew it, I was bawling like a calf in a hailstorm, and there was nobody there to hear me.

When I was all cried out, I got dressed and went to the kitchen. I poured a bowl of cereal and ate at the sink, watching the rain.

Maybe if the sun had been shining, I'd have sat by the pool reading my Sherlock Holmes mystery. Maybe I'd have walked down to the stores on Fairview Drive and pretended to shop for magazines or a new record.

Because of the rain, I discovered Mama's secret.

CHAPTER FIFTEEN

There was no TV in the apartment, and nothing to read except an old movie magazine with Elizabeth Taylor's picture on the cover. I finished reading my Sherlock mystery, made a bologna sandwich for lunch, and thumbed through Mama's sheet music, humming the tunes I knew by heart. After that I got bored and started snooping through the drawers in Mama's dresser. Mixed in with scarves and earrings I remembered from back home were a tangle of stockings, receipts from the Music City Dry Cleaners, a bill for a new tire, and fifty-nine cents in loose change.

In the bottom drawer, hidden way in the back, was a stack of envelopes held together by a rubber band. I opened the first one and a check stub fell out. I looked through the other envelopes. Each one held a check stub from a company called Great Southern Accident and Life. It took me a minute, but then I understood that Mama was cashing the disability checks meant for Opal and me. I sat in front of the open drawer, breathing like I'd just run ten miles, sick with the realization that the people you trust the most may not be what they seem, and what you think is the gospel truth may be nothing but a big fat lie.

The front door opened and Mama called out, "Garnet?"

I fumbled with the envelopes, trying to stuff them back into the drawer. Mama came into the bedroom. "What do you mean, going through my things?"

My rage made me bold. "What do *you* mean, stealing from your own kids?"

"I don't know what you're talking about."

I had to hand it to Mama. She wasn't going down without a fight.

"Daddy's checks," I said. "We've been waiting and waiting for them, living on welfare, wondering why we hadn't got them, and you had them all the time."

Her face closed down and the room felt like the Arctic Ocean, vast and icy cold. "I had to drop everything and go to New Orleans to sign papers for his care," Mama said. "Because of his fool accident, I missed my chance to sing for those music producers. So don't try to make me feel guilty. I'm entitled to that money. It's only fair."

But there was nothing fair about anything that had happened to my family.

"You *left* him!" I reminded her. "Mr. Hancock told Aunt Julia the money was for Opal and me. Do you care that Aunt Julia sold her piano to buy food? That I have to eat sausage and biscuits every single day? Do you know how embarrassing that is?"

Mama shrugged. "I ate plenty of sausage and biscuit lunches when I was your age. It didn't hurt me."

I wanted to say something to hurt her as bad as I was hurting right then. So I told her the truth about the scenery project at school: that I was too ashamed of living in Aunt Julia's run-down house, too ashamed of taking welfare, to accept a ride home after school. But Mama didn't care about my feelings one iota.

"I lived in that house until I was eighteen," she said. "I remember the shame of it. But shame made me tough, and determined to get out of Willow Flats to make something of myself."

She perched on the unmade bed. "I know how you feel. Being poor changes who you are inside. It beats you down and crushes your spirit, and forces you to fight for your dignity every single day of your life."

I gnawed at a cuticle, unwilling to admit she was right. I thought about the kids at the losers' table in the cafeteria, about the way the Barton girls seemed to crawl into a shell whenever anybody looked at them. I thought about my embarrassment at missing that stupid magic show, and the fact that I hid in the bathroom at Aunt Julia's every time the county welfare worker delivered our food box.

Mama went on. "Let's face it. The world is a hard place, Garnet. Nobody gets a break just because of good looks. You're going to have to grow some backbone and go after what you want. If you don't, you'll wind up as roadkill on the great highway of life."

She stood up and stripped off her ketchup-stained waitress uniform. "I smell like grease. Let me wash up and take a nap before we eat. My feet are killing me."

Anger and hurt burned like acid in my blood and choked off my words. It's one thing to tell yourself you're an ugly toad; it's another when your own mother confirms it.

Mama cupped my face in her hand. "Let's have shrimp for dinner. I know it's your favorite." She sounded desperate, like she'd all of a sudden realized she'd messed up really bad and was trying to fix it.

"I'm not hungry."

Her mouth tightened. "Fine. I'd rather sleep than haul you around, anyway." She opened her purse and took out an envelope. "I was going to wait until later to tell you this, but you may as well know now. I got you a ticket back to Oklahoma. The bus leaves tomorrow at nine."

While she showered and napped, I sat at the table remembering the Christmas when I was seven and

Daddy gave me a kaleidoscope. He said the patterns of color and shape were almost as infinite and individual as snowflakes, and that once I turned the cylinder and the pattern changed, I could never get the same one back again. It was the same with Mama. She had arranged all our lives into a whole new pattern, and no matter how bad I wanted to, there could be no going back.

When Mama woke up, we went out for shrimp, but I didn't enjoy a single bite. I sat across from her in a booth at the Surf and Turf, still smarting from her lecture, missing Opal more than I thought was possible, and wishing I was back in Oklahoma. Then she took me to an open mike club, where people could get up and sing whether they had any talent or not. It was a tiny, dark place that smelled like beer and hair spray.

It was obvious Mama went there a lot. When we went in, the owner waved and said, "Hey, Mel."

"Hey, Richie," Mama said. "Okay if I let my little girl sit in tonight?"

"If the cops find out I've got a minor in here, they'll yank my liquor license." He grinned at me. "If I tell you to scram, you scram."

We sat at a table near the back. Mama ordered a Coke for me, but all she had was a glass of water with lemon in it. "To keep my voice limbered up," she said, as the lights came up and a boy in a white cowboy hat three sizes too big ambled onto the stage.

"Hey, ever'body," he drawled, even though there was nobody there except Mama, Richie, me, and a couple of waitresses behind the bar.

The cowboy said, "I'm Dusty Rhodes, and here's a tune made famous by the great Hank Williams." He strummed his guitar and he started wailing about broken promises and cheating hearts and how being unfaithful to your one true love was sure to keep you awake at night.

I stole a glance at Mama. She seemed transported to another place, mouthing the words along with the cowboy, her fingers stroking the edge of her guitar like she was petting a cat. Dusty finished his song. We clapped, and he shuffled off the stage and into the dark.

A couple of men came in. Mama turned around and her mouth dropped open. Her fingernails dug into my arm.

"Ow! What is it, Mama?" I whispered. "Cops?"

"No. Record producers. See that guy with the gray ponytail? That's Ash Wilkins. He's a big shot at RCA. Oh, my lord. I can't believe it! Ash Wilkins!"

Ash and his pal said something to the waitress, then leaned against the bar talking to Richie, who nodded a few times and called, "Hey, Mel. Sing something for these guys, will you?"

Mama grabbed her guitar and gulped water. "Wish me luck, precious."

She ran onto the stage and adjusted the mike. "Hi,

everybody. I'm Melanie McClain, and here's a little song of my own. The story of my life so far. I hope you like it."

She strummed a few chords and sang:

She was seventeen and a beauty queen
On the day they said 'I do.'
They settled down outside of town
In a love nest built for two.
But when the crops all failed
And he got jailed
She decided to try her luck.
With nothin' but a dream and an old guitar
And a 'forty-seven pickup truck.

In my humble opinion, the song was awful. Plus, most of it was lies. It was true Mama married Daddy right after high school, and she *was* the Willow County Strawberry Queen one year, but the only crop my parents ever planted was our vegetable garden out behind the house. Most of all, my daddy had never spent a day of his life in jail. I couldn't believe Mama would make up such a whopper and sing it in front of total strangers.

Mama threw her head back and launched into the second verse. I snuck a peek at the big shots to see how her act was going over. Ash Wilkins had turned his back to the stage and was whispering to one of the girls at the bar. Mama kept singing.

Well, she was wild, she was crazy,
The future looked hazy,
But she wanted to try her luck.
With a pocket full of dreams and an old guitar
And a 'forty-seven pickup truck.

Mama hit a few final chords and bowed, but Ash and his pal had already left. Richie said, "Too bad, Mel. Better luck next week."

"Sure." Mama's voice cracked as she packed her guitar away and snapped the case shut. "Maybe I'll do a Hank Williams number next time."

"Ash Wilkins isn't the only producer in town," Richie said. "You want to hang around a while, see if somebody else shows up?"

"I'm tired," Mama said. "I think I'll call it a night. Besides, I've got Garnet with me."

Mama waved to the bartenders, and we went out to the truck. She started the engine and turned the heater up. "We need to get home and get you packed," she said. "The bus leaves early tomorrow."

But I didn't take the bus back to Willow Flats. When we got home, someone was waiting for us. Mama peered at the dark figure on the doorstep.

"Holy moly!" she yelped. "Julia, is that you?"

CHAPTER SIXTEEN

Mama handed me her guitar case and put her key in the lock. "I swear, Julia, I feel like I'm hosting a family reunion, only somebody forgot to tell me. Where's Opal? Or is she the surprise for tomorrow?"

"Opal is staying with Sunday Larson," Aunt Julia said. "And hello to you, too, Melanie."

"Oh, for heaven's sake." Mama threw the door open and we went in.

Aunt Julia said to me, "Are you okay?"

Before I could open my mouth to answer, she said, "If you ever run off like this again, I'll wear you out, do you understand?"

"I'm sorry I worried you." I set Mama's guitar case down. "I left a note."

"So that makes it all right?" Aunt Julia looked so

frazzled I felt ashamed for what I'd put her through.

Mama tossed her purse onto a kitchen chair. "Lighten up, Julia. She apologized. And there was no use for you to come all this way. I told Sunday I'd send Garnet home on the bus." She squinted at Aunt Julia. "How did you get here, anyway?"

"Borrowed Charlie's car."

I couldn't believe Aunt Julia had driven across three states to bring me back. "Mama said you were afraid to drive!" I blurted. "Because of your accident."

"Nevertheless, I made it," Aunt Julia said proudly. "I didn't get lost even once, unless you count the fruitless trip to that fleabag hotel clear across town." She frowned at Mama. "How come you didn't tell us you'd moved? What if there had been another emergency?"

"I was going to," Mama said, "but I've been busy. Building a career in the music business takes a lot of time."

"Mama's been real busy being a waitress and singing stupid songs to empty rooms," I said to my aunt.

"Right," Aunt Julia said grimly. "Busy taking money from her own children."

Mama cocked her hip and crossed her arms. "So you know."

"Finally," Aunt Julia said. "After umpteen phone calls to poor Mr. Hancock, who must think I am the stupidest woman on the face of the earth. How could I not know the checks were going to my own sister all this time?"

I had never seen Aunt Julia so mad. She snapped her fingers at Mama. "Hand me your purse."

I was stunned at how fast Mama handed it over. Like she was six years old and had got caught stealing from the candy dish. Aunt Julia counted the cash in Mama's wallet and flipped through her checkbook. She added things up in her head and said, "A check for nine hundred dollars should tide us over. Where's your pen?"

"But that's half of what's left in my account!" Mama cried.

"Yes," Aunt Julia said calmly. "I talked to Mr. Hancock yesterday. Apparently there was a mix-up in their accounting office. But it's all straightened out, and from now on the checks will be coming directly to my house for the girls. So I suggest you get famous in a hurry. Your gravy train just left the station."

For a minute none of us said a word, but I could feel that something had changed between Mama and me. And between Aunt Julia and me. Out on Fairview Drive, cars and trucks rushed past, their tires hissing on the pavement. Mama's alarm clock *tick-tick-ticked* too loud in the silence.

"Fine!" Mama said at last. "You don't have to be so mean about it." She scribbled a check and handed it to Aunt Julia, who dropped it into her pocketbook and said, "Garnet, get your things. We're going home."

"Now? In the middle of the night?" Even though Mama and I were mad at each other, I wasn't completely ready to let her go. I hoped she would ask us to stay until morning, but she didn't. I gathered my stuff and met Aunt Julia in the hallway.

Mama cried a little as she kissed me good-bye, but I could see she was relieved, too, and I had to accept that Melanie Hubbard—excuse me, Melanie *McClain*—just wasn't mother material, no matter how badly I needed her to be. Me and Aunt Julia climbed into Charlie's car. She started the engine and switched on the headlights, and we pulled onto the street.

"I'm sorry I worried you," I said when we stopped at a motel for the night. "I was desperate for Mama to come home. I thought if I could talk to her she'd see—"

"Never mind." Aunt Julia pressed her callused hand to my cheek. The love in her touch was an early Christmas present I hadn't even realized I'd wanted.

In the morning, after breakfast at the Pancake Palace, we started off again. As I settled onto the seat beside Aunt Julia, I thought about Celestial and Faith and the tales they would tell about my adventure in Nashville. They were always in on the latest gossip, though they never took blame for spreading it around. But it didn't matter anymore. Despite the way things had turned out with Mama, I was glad she'd shown me the importance of following your heart, even when everything seems totally hopeless.

As the miles slid by, I thought about Powla. I hoped my skipping school hadn't got her into trouble with Mr. Conley. I decided that after I apologized to her I'd try to grow the backbone Mama had talked about and sign up to help with the scenery project. The thought of working with my favorite teacher after school put me in a better frame of mind. I switched on the radio, and me and Aunt Julia sang until the station faded to static and a Spanish station came on. Then Aunt Julia switched it off and said, "If you could pick any one thing from the Sears and Roebuck catalog for Christmas, what would you choose?"

The vast array of possibilities left me momentarily speechless. Finally I said, "Are you serious?"

"Serious as a heart attack," Aunt Julia said. "You girls have had a terrible year. It's time something good happened."

But I wasn't ready to pick a present. There was too much to consider. I leaned my head against the car window, drunk on Christmas dreams.

We got to Willow Flats just after midnight. It looked different in the dark, with shadows softening its sharp edges and a pool of red light from the traffic signal reflecting on the asphalt. We bumped along the road past the courthouse, past the feed store and the Rexall, then headed down to Sunday's place. A lamp glowed in the living room, and the porch light blazed. Before Aunt Julia could turn off the engine, Sunday dashed outside, her polka-dot pajama top billowing out behind her, the laces of her work boots flapping as she ran.

Aunt Julia cranked the window down.

"Opal's gone," Sunday said. "I heard a noise out back and figured the foxes were after my chickens again. I went out to check, and when I came in, I peeked in to see if Opal was awake. Her bed hasn't been slept in. I can't imagine where she's gone."

A chill that had nothing to do with the cold night air started at the back of my spine and skittered all the way up to the top of my head.

Sunday peered through the open car window at me. "Do you know anything about this?"

I had a pretty good idea where my sister was, but I didn't want to rat on her, even if she had been mostly ignoring me lately.

"Garnet, if you know where she's gone, you'd better tell me now," Aunt Julia said. "She could be in trouble. She could get hurt."

I swallowed. "Some of the high school kids meet at a place by the river. To dance and stuff."

"Whereabouts on the river?" Sunday's breath came out in little white puffs.

"I don't know."

"I'll bet it's out past the quarry," she said. "You remember that place, Julia. They closed the road years ago."

"I remember,"Aunt Julia said tiredly.

"Come on," Sunday said, opening the car door. "We'll take my truck. You're too exhausted to drive another mile."

We piled into the cab and Sunday cranked the engine. The truck shook so hard I thought pieces of it might start flying off, but it held together as we sped toward the river until we came to a falling-down wooden gate where the road ended. We twisted and turned along a weedy path until we saw a bonfire flickering in the dark and the dull shine of a bunch of cars parked on the riverbank. Music blared from the radios.

Sunday drove right up to the fire, knocked over a pyramid of empty beer cans, and laid on the horn. The long, earsplitting blast echoed through the trees.

"Hey, cut that out!" a boy yelled. "You want to get the sheriff down here?"

Sunday left the headlights on. She and Aunt Julia got out of the truck. Sunday strode toward the fire and hollered, "Where is Opal Hubbard?"

Through the windshield I could see Opal's two best friends, Cheryl Winslow and Tacy Graves. In the glare of the headlights they looked small and ghostly.

Cheryl said, "Honest, Mrs. Larson, we haven't seen her all night."

Aunt Julia hollered, "Travis Judd? If you're out there, you'd better show yourself, boy."

And, just like Mama giving up her purse, Travis walked out of the shadows. I had to hand it to Aunt Julia. When she said "jump," people jumped. Maybe it was her training as a singer that gave her such a commanding presence. All I know is, it worked.

"Where's my niece?" Aunt Julia demanded.

"She was here," Travis admitted, "but we had a fight and she took off."

"When?"

"I dunno." He ran his fingers through his hair. "A while ago."

"Well, where'd she go?" Sunday asked.

He shrugged. "Home, I guess."

Sunday wheeled on Cheryl and Tacy. "Some friends you are, letting a girl walk home in the dark by herself."

Tacy said, "This isn't the first time she's got mad at Travis and stormed off. She always comes back. Eventually."

"Well, she's not here now," Aunt Julia snapped. "And if a single hair on her head has come to harm, all of you will regret the day you were born."

She and Sunday got back in the truck. Sunday yelled out the window, "Put that fire out and get on home, before I call the law."

Kids appeared from the shadows. Car doors slammed. Engines started up. Sunday turned the truck around and we started back to the road. "Keep an eye out for Opal," she said, and I strained my eyes against the dark woods, looking for my sister. Beside me, Aunt Julia was breathing hard, like she couldn't decide whether to cry or scream.

"Don't panic," Sunday said as we neared our house. "If she's not home, we'll call Sheriff Cates. He'll find her."

Sunday pulled into the yard and we ran inside. The house was dark, the rooms cold. Aunt Julia switched on the living room lamp, and we went upstairs.

My sister was lying on her bed, a quilt pulled up to her chin. The whole room smelled like beer.

Aunt Julia switched on the lamp. "Opal? Are you all right? What happened?"

Opal sniffed. "It's no big deal."

"You ran off in the middle of the night, scared us all half to death, and it's no big deal?"

Sunday said, "Did he hurt you, honey?"

Opal shook her head. But there was a huge red welt on her cheek, and her lip was swollen. "He kept on touching me and kissing me, even after I told him I was scared and begged him to stop. I tried to get away, but he pushed me down on the car seat." Opal gulped. "I hit my cheek on the door handle. Then he got really mad. He called me a tease and a crybaby, and shoved me out of the car."

"You know, Julia, Travis Judd is eighteen years old and Opal is still a minor. You can press charges if you want," Sunday said.

"No!" Opal sat up. "Things are bad enough as they are. Please, Aunt Julia. I'm okay. Let it go."

Aunt Julia said, "I have just driven clear to Nashville and back to retrieve one runaway, and now this. I'm too tired to think right now. But you are not off the hook, Opal Jane. I won't let this slide."

"No, ma'am," Opal said.

Sunday patted Opal's shoulder. "I'd better get on home. I'm glad you're all right."

"I'm sorry," Opal whispered. "I'm sorry I sneaked out on you."

"Me too. There's nothing I hate worse than being lied to. But I reckon you've learned your lesson."

Sunday turned to Aunt Julia. "Leave Charlie's car at my place tonight and return it tomorrow. He won't mind."

"That would be a relief," Aunt Julia said.

"Go on to bed," Sunday said. "I'll be back in the morning."

They went downstairs. I said to Opal, "I didn't tell Aunt Julia you snuck out before, but tonight I had to tell her where to look for you. I was scared."

"It's okay." Opal touched her swollen lip and winced. "I should have known I'd get caught sooner or later."

Then everything caught up with me and I started to cry. Gulping tears, I told Opal everything: how Mama had moved to a fancy apartment without even telling us, how she'd taken the money that was meant for us, how Aunt Julia made Mama give nine hundred dollars of it back.

Opal shook her head. "Boy, I never expected Mama to stoop that low."

Thinking about how Mama had seemed so relieved to see me go made me cry harder. "She's working as a *waitress*! Nobody likes her stupid songs. She's never going to be a star, and she still won't come back!"

"What did you expect? That she would give up everything and come home just because you wanted it?" Opal pulled me down beside her and stroked my head. "You're dumb, but not that dumb."

She lifted the covers and I crawled in beside her, clothes, shoes, and all. While we waited for the house to warm up, I told Opal what Aunt Julia said about picking a Christmas present from the catalog.

"After tonight I probably won't get anything," Opal said. "I just hope she doesn't make me give up my theater arts class." She sighed. "Did you see the way she scowled at me? If looks could kill, I'd be dead by now."

"You scared her," I said. "Even worse than I did by going to Nashville."

"What's Nashville like?" Opal asked. "Is it really better than Mirabeau, like Mama said?"

But I was already drifting off, dreaming of Christmas.

CHAPTER SEVENTEEN

Starch and Vinegar assigned an essay about the Bill of Rights, and everybody groaned. As if school weren't confusing enough, the teachers had been to a workshop about connecting all the different subjects, and now we were writing essays about scientists in Mr. Riley's health class and working math problems about population trends in history class. Personally I liked it better when all the subjects stayed separate, the same way I liked my mashed potatoes to keep their distance from peas and carrots.

It was Friday, with only one more week to go before Christmas vacation, and I couldn't wait to get home and check the mail for our Sears and Roebuck package. After Opal's episode at the quarry with Octopus Boy, Aunt Julia grounded her for a month, with the exception of theater practice, and gave her a bunch of extra chores around the house. But our aunt wasn't heartless enough to deny my sister a Christmas present. Opal and I had spent a week debating what to choose. We nearly wore out the catalog poring over page after page of dresses, shoes, record players, charm bracelets, even a machine that spit out a quart of hot popcorn anytime you wanted it.

At first I had my heart set on a new baseball glove to replace the one I'd left back in Mirabeau, but Opal, who had decided on a pink angora sweater set, said since we'd be going home soon, it would be a waste of good money. Finally I settled on a deluxe set of art supplies in a wooden box. It included colored chalk, watercolors, two camel-hair brushes, and five tubes of oil paint. I longed to see the package waiting for me under the tree that Aunt Julia put up in the living room, in the empty space where her piano used to be.

I was dying to tell Powla about my new supplies. After I'd apologized to her for skipping class, I swallowed my pride and told her I wanted to work on the scenery project more than anything. But she came down with the flu, and we got a substitute teacher before she had a chance to ask Mrs. Brown about giving me a ride home. If I had been brave enough, I would have asked Nathan myself, but every time he looked at me, my tongue stopped working.

"Garnet?" Miss Sparrow said. "Are you with us?"

SEMIPRECIOUS

"Earth to Garnet," Cooley whispered.

"Yes, ma'am, I'm right here."

"Well, then?"

I hadn't heard the question, and Starch and Vinegar was standing there waiting for a brilliant answer. I glanced around wildly for some clue, but the chalkboard, except for the assignment, was bare. Then Nathan thumped his pencil, accidentally on purpose, and it rolled across his desk and fell to the floor. He bent down to retrieve it. As his head came up, he muttered, "Main parts of an essay."

"The main parts of an essay," I recited, "are a topic sentence, supporting arguments, examples, rebuttals, and conclusions."

Cooley's hand was waving wildly in the air. "Miss Sparrow! Miss Sparrow!"

"What is it, Cooley?"

"How long does the essay have to be?"

The bell rang. Out in the hallway, people were laughing, slamming locker doors, hurrying to class before the next bell. But Miss Sparrow leaned against the corner of her desk like she had all the time in the world. "I'll give you the answer Abraham Lincoln gave when someone asked him how long a man's legs should be."

I glanced at Nathan. He grinned and rolled his supergorgeous honey-amber-golden-brown eyes. My stomach jumped. I smiled back.

Miss Sparrow went on. "'A man's legs,' Mr.

215

Lincoln said, 'should be long enough to touch the ground.' Likewise, your essay should be long enough to cover your topic. I expect to see some original thinking here, people, not something copied from a book. Any other questions?"

Nobody said anything, and she let us go.

I stood up, still in shock that Nathan had saved me. I was working up the nerve to actually speak to him, but before I was ready, he sprinted toward the gym with a couple of other boys, and I headed for math class. In all the weeks since I'd apologized for my answer to his train question, Mr. Stanley had hardly said a word to me. I still didn't understand half of what was going on in his class, so I kept my head down and tried to be invisible.

Then, without Powla, art class was a huge waste of time. The sub, Mr. Burrows, didn't know the first thing about art, so he handed out the supplies and told us to do whatever we wanted. I went to the cabinet where our works in progress were kept, and took out the watercolor I was working on for Daddy's Christmas present, a picture of our house in Mirabeau in the springtime, when the trees are busting out in green and the daffodils are blooming. But my hands decided to separate from my brain, and the next thing I knew, I was doodling Nathan Brown's name all over a sheet of drawing paper. My hand made hearts and flowers and curlicues and tried drawing his face, but it couldn't do justice to his amazing eyes. I watched him standing at the easel, chewing his bottom lip and smearing green paint, Picasso-style, onto a canvas. Totally adorable.

"Where is Garnet Hubbard?" Mr. Burrows fumbled with his glasses and squinted at Powla's seating charts. After a week of substituting, you'd think he would have learned a few of our names, but it was like he woke up in a brand-new world every morning.

I raised my hand.

Mr. Burrows said, "Would you take the attendance report to the office, please? And ask Mrs. Wink for more drawing paper. I'm running low for next period."

I left my stuff on my desk, went to the office, and got back to the art room just as the bell rang and disaster struck.

Davis Truluck, one of Nathan's friends, grabbed my paper and waved it in the air. He put his hand over his heart, fluttered his eyelashes, and cooed, "Ohhh, Nathan! I loooove you!"

Mr. Burrows just stood there befuddled while everybody laughed. Everybody except Nathan, who was glaring at me, silent death rays shooting out of his eyes.

"Give me back my paper!" I grabbed it out of Davis's hands and ran to the restroom, where I stayed all during lunch, bawling my eyes out. How could I have been stupid enough to think Nathan liked me? I could imagine Celestial and Faith laughing at me and spreading the story all over school. I leaned against the wall and prayed for death, but when the last lunch bell rang, I was still alive. I washed my face and went to my locker. A rolled-up piece of paper was wedged into the door.

>*Dear Garnet,*
>*Nathan Brown said to tell you he hates you. A lot.*
>*Signed, a friend*

I stumbled through the rest of the day in a fog of mortified despair. When the bus came, I climbed on for the long ride home. I wanted my sister, but Opal was staying late for play practice. I turned my face to the window, swallowing my tears. It didn't matter so much that Nathan hated me; everybody in the whole miserable school hated me. But now I wouldn't dare ask him for a ride. Sometimes you just know that something is supposed to be yours. Art was meant to be mine, and being shut out of the scenery project made it seem farther away than ever.

When the bus stopped at our house, I could see there was no package from Sears and Roebuck waiting for me, but I'd had such a horrible day I no longer cared. Charlie's car was parked in the yard, though, and that almost made up for the empty mailbox. A visit from Charlie was a different kind of present.

He was sitting in front of the fire in the living

room, having coffee and cake with Aunt Julia. He smiled when I dumped my books on the coffee table. "Garnet Hubbard."

"Hey, Charlie."

"I heard you took a little trip." Charlie looked at me in that way he had that made me feel like he could see every thought running through my brain.

"The worry dolls told me to go. But nothing worked out the way it was supposed to."

He sipped his coffee and stared into the fire.

Aunt Julia said, "Guess what came today?"

She pointed to two packages wrapped in silver paper lying under the Christmas tree. I didn't want to disappoint her, so I pretended I was the most excited kid in the universe. I ran over to the tree, picked up my package, and shook it, like I was trying to guess what was inside.

"Careful!" Aunt Julia said. "You may need that for your scenery project at school."

"How did you know about that?"

Charlie handed me a piece of blue notepaper that smelled like flowers. "This came from your mother this morning."

> Dear Charlie,
>
> I hope you remember me. I am Julia's younger sister. I'm writing to thank you for lending Julia your car and to ask you for another huge favor. My daughter Garnet has a chance to work on an important project at

school, but she has no way of getting home after the bus
runs. Would you consider giving her a ride? I don't have
much money, but I can pay a small amount each week.
Because this is so important to Garnet, it's important to
me, too, and I hope you can see your way clear to help
us out. Thanks a bunch!

Melanie McClain

I was dumbfounded. After everything that had happened in Nashville, the last thing I expected from
Mama was kindness.

Charlie just sat there, watching me. He reminded
me of the raptors we'd studied in science class last year,
and the way they stay still for hours, saving their energy
until it's needed for something important. Charlie was
an eagle. Quiet, watchful, still.

Aunt Julia said, "Charlie is willing to give you a
ride as long as you don't stay too late."

He nodded. "I don't see so well at nighttime anymore."

"I promise!" I hugged Aunt Julia first, and then
Charlie.

He stood and picked up his hat. "I'm going now,
Julia," he said. "I hear the river calling."

Aunt Julia smiled. "You be careful out there. It's
chilly today, and you're not as young as you used to be."

Charlie nodded gravely. "I won't stay out long.
Good-bye, Garnet Hubbard."

"Bye, Charlie! I'll let you know what days to pick me up, okay?"

He waved one hand in my general direction and let himself out.

I stood there grinning like an idiot. I couldn't believe that something good had finally happened in Willow Flats. Something so great I didn't care that Nathan Brown hated me, or that Celestial and Faith would spread the news of my art class episode all over seventh grade by the time the first bell rang on Monday.

Aunt Julia read Mama's note again, like she couldn't believe it either. "This is the first unselfish thing your mother has done since she made a pot holder for me in third grade."

It seemed like a miracle. Mama actually understood that I wanted a life in art as much as she wanted to be the next Cordell Jackson. When she sent me back from Nashville, I'd tried to let go, but blood is a thread that connects you to other people, no matter what.

Opal got home from play practice ten minutes before her curfew, just as darkness came. Aunt Julia switched on the lamp, and we ate sandwiches in front of the fire, listening to a performance of Handel's *Messiah* broadcast from a church in Tulsa. When the fire burned low, I went out to the porch for more wood.

It had begun to snow; huge flakes tumbled and glittered in the porch light. I sent a bunch of silent thank-yous into the night. To all the doctors in New Orleans who were putting my daddy back together, to Miss Mendez for encouraging my dream, and to Mama for understanding how badly I wanted it.

Aunt Julia came out, and we stood there until our fingers went numb, watching a curtain of moonlight steal across the new snow.

Chapter Eighteen

By the time the last day before Christmas vacation finally dawned, even the teachers stopped pretending anybody was going to learn anything. Miss Sparrow gave up on trying to teach us the difference between active voice (I hate Willow Flats School) and passive voice (Willow Flats School is hated by me) and read to us from "A Child's Christmas in Wales." I listened to Mr. Dylan Thomas's description of how his Christmas was full of useful presents like earmuffs and mittens, and useless ones like jelly babies, whistles, and hatchets. How on Christmas morning, with his house full of uncles and aunts, he'd go out to play in the snow with his friends. I wished for such a Christmas for Opal and me, but this year it would be just Aunt Julia and the two of us, and one lonely present apiece under our lopsided Christmas tree.

In math Mr. Stanley handed out a worksheet of problems like any regular day, but they were Christmas-themed problems and printed on green paper. In art class Powla decided we needed a break from Diego Rivera and the muralists. She brought in her collection of spun-glass ornaments and showed some slides of the glassblowers at work. At lunch the cafeteria ladies wore red Santa hats and went around to each table, handing out green and red sugar cookies shaped like stars and Christmas trees.

Miss Browning tried to make history relevant by talking about the evolution of Christmas traditions around the world, but most people were too keyed up to pay attention. We were waiting for sixth period, when classes would be canceled and we could watch the ninth graders' Christmas pageant. Naturally, Opal had the biggest part. She was the Head Angel, narrating the story of the birth of Jesus and the visit of the Three Wise Men. Aunt Julia had sewn her costume, a long white robe with feathered wings. Opal wore one of Mama's beauty-queen crowns to serve as a halo. I knew Opal had been practicing a dramatic stage entrance in secret, but all she'd tell me was that it was sure to make this performance her most memorable one ever.

After fifth-period classes were over, everybody filed into the auditorium, and the classes broke up into their usual clans. Celestial and Faith and their religious friends commandeered the front row so that Faith, with her superior biblical knowledge, could be sure Opal told the Jesus story straight. Next came the athletes. Nathan dropped into a seat right behind Celestial's and slid so far down nobody could see his face. The seventh-grade cheerleaders, dressed alike in red corduroy jumpers and white blouses, sat behind the jocks. As usual, I sat alone.

Mr. Riley leaned against the wall talking to Powla, no doubt giving her some tips on how to avoid getting the flu again by washing her hands more often. Behind me the eighth graders came in, pushing and trading good-natured cursing, until Principal Conley came in and grabbed one of them by the shirt.

"What was that you said, mister?"

"Nothing, sir."

"Nothing my eye. If this wasn't Christmas, I'd haul you to detention. Watch your mouth, Ricky." He scanned the rows of upturned faces. "That goes for all of you. Remember that the behavior of one reflects upon all Willow Flats Warriors. Let's build a school we can be proud of."

I half expected him to pull out a set of pom-poms and yell, "Rah!" but he moved on to harass someone else. The high schoolers came in and took their seats. The curtain opened and a spotlight came on. The choir shuffled onto the stage, opened their red music folders, and started humming "Silent Night," mostly on key.

Backstage there was a thud, and then Opal appeared in her costume. A pair of hands came out from behind the curtain and gave Opal a push. As she glided toward the center of the stage, her feathered wings moving up and down, I realized she was wearing roller skates under her robe. The sound of the wheels thundered in the hushed auditorium as Opal rolled across the stage. *Thump-thump, thump-thump.*

I didn't mean to laugh. It came out before I could stop it, a burst of sound like a gunshot. The cheerleaders turned around and stared. Cooley snickered, then laughter spread across the auditorium faster than a new piece of gossip.

Opal didn't lose her composure. She stopped center stage, raised her angel's wings, and began in a loud voice, "And it came to pass in those days, that there went out a decree from Caesar Augustus, that all the world should be taxed."

But the laughter got louder and more hysterical until she turned around, her face flaming, and skated off, the wheels of her skates slamming against the floor. The choir stopped humming.

The seniors whistled and stomped their feet. Mr. Conley ran onto the stage and grabbed the microphone. "All right, people, settle down."

The choir director covered the mike with her hands

and spoke to Mr. Conley, who nodded and said something back.

The ninth graders began to chant, "O-pal! O-pal!"

A spit wad smacked the back of my head. Cooley was out of his seat, dancing in the aisle. The ninth-grade cheerleaders were yelling, "Gooooooo, Opal!"

Coach Riley pulled out his whistle and blew directly into the microphone. That got people's attention. Then Mr. Conley took over and said how disappointed he was at our behavior, and how we had proved we weren't ready to take our places in civilized society, blah blah blah. He sent us all back to our sixth-period classes to wait for the last bell.

Another spit wad pinged my face. I looked up. The boy who had called me a swamp rat back on the first day of school said, "You stupid creep! Why'd you have to go and ruin everything?"

Celestial and Faith pushed past me. "Nice going, Garnet," Faith said. "I didn't realize how jealous you were."

Celestial nodded. "You should make an effort to make something of yourself, instead of sabotaging your sister just because she's cute and popular."

I doubled up my fist and was a tenth of a second from smacking them both right in the mouth when Powla appeared like a fairy godmother and said, "Garnet, I need your help in the art room."

I followed behind her as she plowed through the

crowd like a ship cutting through waves. In the art room she nudged the door shut, pulled out a chair, and said, "I'm sorry for what happened just now, but you can't let those girls push you into a fight. If they get you into trouble, then they win."

"I hate them," I said.

"That's a strong word."

"It's true, though. They think they are so much better than me."

"Are they?"

"No!"

"Well, then. What they think doesn't really matter, does it?" The corners of her mouth turned up into a smile. "Does it, Garnet?"

"I guess not."

She got up, went to her desk, and picked up a tiny glass ornament with stars painted on it. "Teachers aren't supposed to have favorites, but you and I have been kindred spirits since the first day. Yes?"

I was so surprised I couldn't say anything right then. I nodded.

She placed the ornament in my hand. "Our little secret, okay?"

"Okay. Thank you, Miss Mendez. I'll keep it forever."

"I hope so."

I stood up. "I should go to class before I get into trouble with Mr. Riley."

"He knows you're with me." Powla glanced at her watch. "The bus will be here in a few minutes. You may as well stay here till then."

She took a key from her pocket and unlocked a door next to the art room. I expected a storeroom or a janitor's closet, but it was a little studio furnished with a chair and a table covered with brushes, tubes of paint, and cans of turpentine. Half-finished paintings and blank canvases leaned against the walls. On an easel was a large painting of a street scene in Mexico, with dark-haired women in flowing skirts, children playing, and flower vendors with their carts.

I thought it was magnificent, like something you'd see in a museum, but when Powla saw me studying it, she waved her hand and said, "It's a failure."

"It's beautiful," I said.

"It's all right technically, but I can't capture irony the way Rivera does. That's the secret to creating something that lasts."

I had no idea what she was talking about.

"The difference between a good painting and a great one is meaning," Powla said, as if she were lecturing to the whole class and not just to one miserable messed-up seventh grader. "A great painting joins the individual to the world by taking something that is painful, or frightening, or mysterious, and turning it into something beautiful. When you look at this picture, what does it say to you?"

"I don't know."

"Exactly."

The bell rang. Doors slapped open, feet thundered down the stairs. Lockers slammed, people shouted. At last, school was out for the holidays.

Powla picked up her keys, and her armload of silver bracelets jingled. "Merry Christmas, Garnet," she said. "See you next year!"

"Merry Christmas." I put my ornament in my sweater pocket and headed for the stairs.

When I got on the bus, everybody stared at me like I'd drowned their pet kittens. Opal brushed past me carrying her skates, her costume, and Mama's crown, and sat by herself too. The bus was quiet as a tomb. Sunday frowned at us in her mirror, then shrugged and tuned her radio to a station playing Christmas songs. While Bing Crosby sang about a white Christmas, I was trying to figure out how to apologize to my sister for ruining her big moment.

The bus rattled along the road. At every stop Sunday called out, "Merry Christmas!" or "See you next year!" to whoever was getting off. When she stopped at our mailbox, though, she said, "Good luck, Garnet."

Nothing ever got past Sunday.

I knew putting off my apology would only make things worse, so as I walked to the house with Opal, I said, "I'm really sorry. I didn't mean to cause a riot."

Opal looked at me like I was pond scum. She marched into the house, threw her costume onto the sofa, and went to the kitchen. She poured a glass of milk, slammed the fridge door shut, and went upstairs. Aunt Julia set her mixing bowl down. "What's the matter with her?"

I explained how the sound of Opal's skates thumping across the stage had set me to laughing, and how Mr. Conley had canceled the performance and everybody blamed me, even though they were all laughing just as hard as I was. "I said I'm sorry, but Opal won't even talk to me."

"Give her some time," Aunt Julia said. "She'll come around."

But I couldn't stand for Opal to stay mad at me for one second. I never could, even when we were little kids. I went upstairs to our room. Opal was lying on her bed playing possum. I stood there feeling the silence, growing more hopeless by the minute. "Say something."

"Okay. I hate you. How's that?"

"I *said* I was sorry. What else can I do?"

"Let's see. Move to another planet? Planet of the Losers."

Then she began to cry. For the first time since Mama had left us, Opal sobbed and sobbed, and I realized that despite having a million friends and being beautiful and popular, deep down she was just like me, desperately wanting our old life back—the one thing she could never have.

I wished her tears would blow away like snowflakes, swirling above the rooftops and the river, but sadness had moved in and plopped itself down like an unwanted relative, and there was nothing I could do to make it go away.

Opal sat up and wiped her eyes. "You're still here."

"Don't be mad at me." I nudged her and sat down on the edge of her bed. "I wasn't laughing at you. It was the sound of the skates that set me off. Where did you get them, anyway?"

"They were in a trunk in the attic. There's all sorts of stuff up there. Old newspapers, a box of opera recordings, even an old Victrola, but I don't think it works." Opal sniffed. "I wanted to rig a harness and fly across the stage, but Miss Barnes said it was too dangerous. Gliding in on skates seemed like the next best thing."

"It was a good idea," I said. "It would have worked, except for the hollow wooden floor."

"It *was* loud, wasn't it?" A smile tugged at the corners of her mouth.

"Loud as a cannon going off."

"Was it really that bad?"

"Not as bad as the time you puked right in the middle of your fifth-grade dance recital."

"Shut up."

"You shut up."

Opal scooted across the bed and bumped me with her hip, and I saw that she was grinning. "Go on," she said. "Leave me alone. I want to be by myself for a while."

I wrapped Powla's ornament in a pair of my socks and stashed it in the suitcase under the bed. I took my sketchbook down to the kitchen table and finished making studies for my history painting, never dreaming my picture would lead to big trouble.

Chapter Nineteen

I sent Daddy's watercolor picture to the hospital along with a Christmas card filled with happy lies. I figured he had more than enough to worry about without knowing how lonely and miserable I felt, so I told him everything was just swell at good old Willow Flats Junior High. I sent Mama a card with a drawing inside and a note thanking her for arranging my ride with Charlie. For Aunt Julia, Opal, Sunday, and Charlie, I made origami crane ornaments—a trick I'd learned when we studied Japan in sixth grade. I sprinkled the cranes with glitter and attached them to gold ribbons I found in Aunt Julia's sewing basket. I made one for Powla, too, even though I wouldn't see her until after Christmas.

I know what you're thinking. A paper crane is the

dumbest possible present for a fourteen-year-old sister, but I still owed Sunday the twenty I'd borrowed for
the Nashville fiasco, and I didn't want to ask Aunt Julia
for money. I was counting on Opal to understand.

On Christmas Eve we were in the kitchen baking
cookies when Sunday's truck roared into the yard. The
snow had melted, leaving behind a sea of red mud.
Sunday slogged across it and jumped onto the porch.
"Hey, Julia!" she yelled. "You home?"

Aunt Julia wiped her hands and opened the door.
"Of course we're home. Where else would we be?"

"There's no telling, since you took up driving again."
Sunday scraped the mud off her boots and handed Aunt
Julia a large cardboard box sealed with tape. "This came
for the girls this morning all the way from Mirabeau. I
figured you'd want it in time for Christmas."

"Mirabeau?" Opal nudged Mozart aside and
elbowed her way to the door. "Let me see."

I could tell she was hoping the package was from
her long-lost love, Waymon Harris, or maybe from
Linda. But the box was addressed to both of us, and the
handwriting was thin and spidery.

"Let's open it!" I said.

"It isn't Christmas yet," Aunt Julia teased. "Don't
you want to wait?"

"No, ma'am," I said. "I love Nancy Drew and
Sherlock Holmes, but I can't stand a real-life mystery,
and I can't figure out who this is from."

"My lands!" Aunt Julia said to Sunday. "Where are our manners? Come in and have coffee. I just made a fresh pot."

"I can't stay," Sunday said. "I haven't finished packing for my trip to Dallas yet." She fished her keys from her pocket. "Polly is looking after things while I'm gone. If you need anything, ask her to put it on your tab."

"Thanks," said Aunt Julia, "but we're fine now. Have a good time. And Merry Christmas."

"To you, too," Sunday said. "Bye, girls!"

"Wait!" I handed Sunday her ornament. "I made this for you."

"Well, isn't that pretty? Thank you, Garnet."

She hopped off the porch. Before she could turn her truck around and drive off, me and Opal had that package opened. On top was a letter from Daddy.

My dear daughters,

Thank you for the beautiful Christmas presents. I have put Garnet's painting on my bedside table where I can see it first thing every morning, and Opal's poem inside my Bible where I can read it every night before I go to sleep. I didn't realize I had two such talented girls!

Since the doctors wouldn't let me out of here to go Christmas shopping, I asked Mrs. Streeter to send you some of your favorite things left behind when your mother took off with you in such a hurry last summer. I hope these

will do until May, when I'll be out of this place for good.
Love and Merry Christmas from Daddy

We dug through the wadded-up newspaper, and there was my fielder's glove, my baseball card collection, and Opal's phonograph and record collection. Opal lifted the phonograph out of the box like she'd just discovered the Holy Grail.

We set it on the coffee table and plugged it in. Opal sorted through her forty-fives and pulled out her favorites. She turned up the volume full blast, and me and Opal danced the bop and the stroll and the twist.

"Come on, Aunt Julia!" Opal said when we put on the Chubby Checker song for the third time. "Do the twist!"

"Oh, I don't think so," Aunt Julia said.

"It's easy," I told her. "If *I* can do it, anybody can."

Then Aunt Julia joined in, laughing with us and singing along with Chubby until she got winded and collapsed on the couch, fanning herself with her apron.

After supper Aunt Julia read the Christmas story and we listened to carols on the radio. When "Silent Night" came on, Mama's favorite, we all three got teary-eyed, but we didn't talk about her. The Christmas card she'd sent the week before sat on the fireplace mantel, as impersonal as the ones we'd got from the garden supply store and the Rexall.

At midnight Aunt Julia gave us our presents and we ripped the silver paper off the boxes and admired them like they were the biggest surprises we'd ever laid eyes on. Opal modeled her sweater set, and I sorted through my paint box, planning pictures in my head.

Aunt Julia said my paper crane was the finest one she'd ever seen, and she found a place for it on our tree. When I gave Opal hers, she said, "It's too pretty to use only at Christmas. I'll hang it over the mirror in our room."

She ran upstairs and came back smiling. She handed Aunt Julia a poem she'd written on pale blue paper, then said to me, "Hold out your hand."

She dropped something round and smooth into my palm.

"Lipstick?"

"It's called Cotton Candy, and it's perfect for you." She took the cap off the tube. "Hold still."

I opened my lips and Opal smoothed on the lipstick.

"You look pretty, Garnet," my sister said.

And that was the best Christmas present of all.

CHAPTER TWENTY

"Scott and Joey, give us a hand with these panels, will you?" Powla motioned to the two sophomore hoodlums slouching in the corner.

The play was now only two weeks away, and we were working fast to get everything done. Nathan had decided to concentrate on baseball training, which left Celestial Jones, Polly Barton, Cindy Lawless, and me to do most of the work. Celestial avoided me like I was the Cootie Queen, but Polly, who was a way better artist than any of the rest of us, smiled at me now and then when Powla offered us a compliment.

Scott and Joey shuffled across the stage and hoisted one of the panels. Scott growled, "Where to?"

The week before, Mr. Conley had caught him and Joey smoking in the restroom and offered them a plea bargain: help us with the scenery project every Tuesday and Thursday after school, or flunk tenth grade. Even with their limited brain power, they could see the choice was simple, so there they were. Sometimes I thought Powla made them move stuff back and forth more than was necessary, just to teach them a lesson.

Miss Barnes, the senior adviser, had chosen readings from *Spoon River Anthology* by Edgar Lee Masters, and according to Powla, it had caused a bigger stink in the teacher's lounge than Mr. Conley's cigars. Miss Sparrow argued that most of the anthology, which consisted of short monologues from a hundred-and-something dead people telling what awful lives they'd had, was too depressing, and we should do *Our Town* by Thornton Wilder instead. Miss Barnes argued that every school between Willow Flats and Sydney, Australia, had done *Our Town* to death and it was time for something different. Miss Barnes won, and now we were finishing the scenes we'd begun last fall, painting Spoon River, Illinois, the way it looked in the old days, with houses and churches in the background, and the river and a graveyard covered with tombstones in the foreground. Polly was in charge of painting the river. I worked on houses and helped Cindy paint the tombstones. Celestial, who couldn't draw a straight line even with the help of a ruler, was in charge of keeping track of our supplies, sweeping up, and lettering SPOON RIVER ANTHOLOGY onto a banner to hang above the stage.

Opal had auditioned and won a part in the play, even though most of the other actors were juniors and seniors. She was to portray Constance Hately, a Spoon River woman who had raised her older sister's daughters. Every night up in our room Opal practiced in front of the mirror, trying out different ways of reciting her last lines. "'But praise not my self-sacrifice. I reared them. I cared for them, true enough! But I poisoned my benefactions with constant reminders of their dependence!'"

Opal was planning to wear one of Aunt Julia's dresses, a pair of old-fashioned ladies' boots, and a bonnet. I was fairly sure she wouldn't rise from the grave on roller skates.

"Okay, everybody, let's stop and clean up," Powla said. "Remember, we have only three more sessions before the dress rehearsal, so it's important that you be here every time, and on time."

Joey grabbed his leather jacket. "Can me and Scotty go now?"

"As soon as you put the paints in the closet. And pick up those drop cloths. I don't want anyone tripping over them."

We all pitched in to help clear the stage. I cleaned the paintbrushes and put away the turpentine.

Powla put the folded drop cloths into the cubbyhole behind the stage. "By the way, Garnet," she said, "how is your painting for your history project coming along? I haven't seen it since you completed your sketches."

"Almost done. It's due in three weeks."

"I'm looking forward to seeing it."

Part of me couldn't wait to show it to her, even though the thought of it made me nervous. I desperately wanted her approval, and I was afraid I'd disappoint her.

Powla stepped back and let out a yelp when she nearly tripped over a broom lying on the stage floor. "Who left this broom here? Celestial?"

Celestial went all wide-eyed innocent. "I don't know! Garnet had it last!"

She was such an actress she should have been in the play.

"I did not!" I shot back. "Sweeping is your job!"

"Girls," Powla said. "Never mind. Just be more careful in the future." She picked up her book bag and started switching off the stage lights.

"Teacher's pet!" Celestial spat. "Commie teacher's pet."

"She's not a Commie. And I never touched that stupid broom and you know it."

"Drop dead twice."

"Ditto." I got my stuff and went outside to wait for Charlie.

As I turned the corner by the gym, I ran right into Nathan Brown. Since getting the hate mail in my locker, I'd gone out of my way to avoid him, so you could have knocked me over with a straw when he said, "Hey, Garnet."

Gosh, his eyes were amazing. I managed to say, "Hey."

He tossed his baseball back and forth, smacking it into his glove. "How's the painting going?"

"Okay."

He nodded. "That's what I figured."

"I'm waiting for my ride."

"Yeah."

"Well, I'll see you in the funny papers."

"Yeah."

A horn honked, and Charlie pulled into the drive. I opened the car door.

"Garnet?" Nathan said. "The season opener is on Saturday. You could come, if you want."

I was too amazed to say a word. I nodded, dumped my books on the floorboard, and got in the car. Nathan stepped back and I closed the door.

"The sun is strong today," Charlie said as we pulled away from the school. "Summer will come early this year, I think."

"I hope so," I said. "My daddy is getting out of the hospital as soon as it warms up. Then we'll go home."

"No place like home," Charlie agreed. He rolled his window down, and the cool spring air blew in. Watching Charlie steer around the potholes the March rains had made, I got the feeling something was wrong, like he had gone off to a whole other place.

"Guess what?" I said. "Nathan Brown invited me to his baseball game."

Charlie nodded. "I'm glad you're making friends."

"Aunt Julia says you've been her friend her whole life."

"We've seen a lot of life together. But our journey is nearly done."

My heart fluttered like a trapped bird. I didn't want to hear what he was trying to say.

Charlie pulled into Aunt Julia's yard and turned to me, his old eyes clouded and wet. "In a little while I will be gone from you."

"Don't say that!"

"Leaving the earth is not a bad thing," Charlie said. "It's time. My spirit wants to be free."

I fumbled for the door handle, desperate to get out of the car before I started to cry. I grabbed my books, slammed the door, and ran inside. Charlie's ancient voice followed me. "Good-bye, Garnet Hubbard."

Aunt Julia was in the garden out back, installing her new whirligigs. I watched them spinning in the breeze, and tried to decide whether or not to tell her what Charlie had said. I'd once seen a documentary on TV about how some people can tell when they're going to die, but I hadn't really believed it. I told myself Charlie would live another ten years, maybe even longer. Some people lived to be a hundred, didn't they? Charlie wasn't even ninety yet.

But he died the next day.

I had just got home from school and was upstairs changing clothes when I saw the Preachermobile coming down the road. When it stopped in the yard and Reverend Underwood climbed out, dressed in his black suit, I knew.

I sat on the stairs and listened to the preacher's conversation with Aunt Julia. "Charlie said you're the closest to family he had. He's left you his car. He said you would know how he wanted his service conducted."

Aunt Julia dabbed at her eyes with a wad of tissue. Mozart leapt into her lap and curled himself around her. "Charlie loved that plot of land near the river. We'll put him there."

"I'll see to it."

They went on talking about flowers and hearses, but I couldn't listen. It was hard to think I would never see Charlie again, that I wouldn't hear any more about worry dolls and spirit dreams, about how he loved sleeping under the stars at night, and how paddling on the river with fish and birds for company was the highest kind of prayer.

The funeral was held on Saturday, and almost everyone in Willow Flats came to say good-bye. After Reverend Underwood read from the Bible, different people stood up and told their favorite stories about Charlie. Sunday

Larson told about the time her barn caught on fire and Charlie was the first one there to help put out the blaze. Cooley's father said Charlie was the one who taught him to hunt, and Miss Sparrow said Charlie lent her a hundred dollars to start college, and without him she never would have become a teacher. Which just goes to show that even Charlie could make an occasional mistake.

I held tight to Opal's hand and thought about the way Charlie had tried to comfort me when Daddy got hurt, how he had given me the bird carving and helped Aunt Julia track Mama down. He had driven me home twice a week without ever making me feel like he was doing me a huge favor. He was one of the best people I'd ever known, but I couldn't stand up and talk about him. I was crying too hard.

Cooley came over and blinked at me through his thick glasses. "I'm real sorry about Charlie Twelvetrees," he whispered. "I know he was your friend."

I waited for the punch line, but Cooley patted my shoulder and went to stand with his parents.

After Ida Wink sang the Lord's Prayer, we walked across the new spring grass to Charlie's coffin. On the way I heard Ida telling Miss Sparrow about plans for a garage sale, and Cooley's dad complaining to the bank manager about the price of seed corn, like they had already forgotten Charlie and were moving on without him.

"Garnet?" The reverend handed me an envelope as

we waited for everyone to gather. "I found this at Charlie's place. It's addressed to you."

I opened the envelope, and the money Mama had sent him to pay for my ride—a wad of crumpled five-dollar bills—fell out. The sight of it sent me into another fit of tears.

"Shhh, it's okay." Opal put her arm around my shoulders and handed me a tissue. "Charlie wouldn't want you to cry about it."

Revered Underwood took his place under the green funeral home tent. The wind whipped his hair and stirred the yellow roses covering Charlie's coffin. "Not long ago," he began, "Charlie told me that when the time came, he wanted to say good-bye with this prayer of his ancestors." The preacher took a piece of paper from his prayer book and read, "Great Spirit, whose voice whispers in the wind, whose breath is the breath of life to all the world, hear my prayer. Let me live strong, as the buffalo is strong. Let me light the world as the firefly lights the summer night, and when my time on Earth is finished, let the raven bear my spirit skyward, that I may return to you without shame."

I closed my eyes and imagined Charlie paddling his canoe on the water, the fireflies darting and flashing in the darkness. I imagined the stirring of the wind in the willow trees and Charlie's oars whispering to the river.

High above me, a black-winged bird circled the river, rising higher and higher until it was lost in the sun.

CHAPTER TWENTY-ONE

Because of Charlie's funeral, I missed Nathan's baseball game. Opal said it was good that I hadn't gone to the game, because boys are more interested in you when you play hard to get. The next Monday in homeroom, while Miss Sparrow's back was turned, Nathan opened a brand-new package of peppermints and offered me the first one, so I guess maybe my sister knows a thing or two about dealing with the opposite sex.

Now that she had Charlie's car, Aunt Julia took to driving again like a duck to water. She went to the courthouse and signed some papers that said the car was truly hers. She kept the roads hot between school, the Texaco, and Sunday's place, and when Mozart got a hair ball roughly the size of Dallas, she drove him to the animal hospital in Hopkinsville.

The night of the spring play Opal put her makeup and costume into our suitcase and Aunt Julia drove us to school. In the parking lot she twisted around in her seat and said to Opal, "Break a leg."

Opal grinned. "I'll wait for you by the stage door after, okay?"

Inside, the auditorium buzzed with sound. Aunt Julia and I found seats near the back and saved one for Sunday Larson. Reverend Underwood and his wife came in, and Aunt Julia waved to them. Ida Wink patted my shoulder as she came down the aisle with Mr. Conley and Coach Riley. Cooley was there with his parents. Nathan came in with his mother and took a seat close to the front. Celestial Jones, in a hot-pink dress and matching shoes with tiny heels, started down the aisles, handing out programs to everyone, smiling like she'd just been crowned Miss America.

When she got to me, she held a program out with two fingers, like she was afraid touching me would give her malaria.

Aunt Julia said, "Garnet tells me you helped with the scenery for the play."

"Yes, ma'am," Celestial said. "I painted the banner. A very important job."

Then Sunday came in and plopped into the seat we'd saved for her. "Sorry I'm late! I got tied up in town."

The house lights dimmed and the stage lights

blazed on. Loud whispers came from behind the stage curtain. Then the senior class adviser, Miss Barnes, stepped onto the stage, welcomed everyone to the play, and said, "Now I'd like to introduce our art teacher, Miss Paula Mendez."

Powla read the names of everybody who had helped with the scenery project. "These students worked many hours after school to recreate the town of Spoon River, Illinois, as it might have looked in the last century. Our title banner was created by Celestial Jones."

Little Miss Perfect stood up, turned, and waved as the curtain parted and the banner was lowered into place. It said SOON RIVER ANTHOLOGY.

"Hey, Celestial," somebody called. "You forgot your *P*!" It sounded like the delinquent Joey Davis, but I couldn't be sure because his next words were drowned in laughter. Celestial ran out of the auditorium, the door banging shut behind her.

The audience settled down. Opal stood near the right side of the stage as the other players recited the parts of Mrs. Kessler, Elizabeth Childers, and Faith Matheny.

Then my sister stepped into the spotlight. "You praise my self-sacrifice, Spoon River," she began, and it seemed like the whole audience was holding its breath. I remembered last spring, back in Mirabeau, when she'd played Juliet so convincingly that half the audience cried. Tonight Opal looked more beautiful than ever, serene and far away, just the way Mama looked when she was playing her guitar. The stage was a refuge for Opal, too. As long as she was pretending to be someone else, she didn't have to worry about Daddy's injuries or wonder whether Mama was ever coming home.

It would have been easy to feel jealous of Opal, of her beauty and her talent, but I knew that a life in art was meant to be mine, if only I was brave enough to go after it. I wouldn't end up like Aunt Julia, standing on the sidelines, watching someone else play the game.

Opal's part was ending. "But I poisoned my bene-factions with constant reminders of their dependence!"

Aunt Julia found my hand in the dark and squeezed it hard. I squeezed back.

The play went on, and like Miss Sparrow had argued, the stories the Spoon River dead people told were pretty grim. They were stories of dead children, lost wives, deep regrets, and missed opportunities. All in all, pretty depressing.

When the last story ended, the whole cast stepped forward and bowed. Applause erupted around us as the house lights came up. We clapped and clapped as Opal and the other cast members left the stage, then ran back on for another bow. Aunt Julia, Sunday, and I chatted as we waited for the aisles to empty. Then Sunday left to talk to Ida Wink, and me and Aunt Julia pushed through the crowd to the stage door to wait for

Opal. A knot of parents and teachers spilled down the stairs and across the hall. Celestial, red-faced and teary-eyed, rushed past us.

Powla appeared at my side, her dark eyes snapping with excitement. "I'm so proud of your work, Garnet. The whole evening went very well, don't you think?"

"Yes, ma'am. Except that Celestial's banner was misspelled."

"Yes," Powla said. "That was unfortunate, but Celestial insisted she didn't need me looking over her shoulder while she worked." She shrugged. "And so she pays a price for her hubris."

I wasn't sure what "hubris" meant, but I could see that Miss Mendez wasn't exactly feeling sorry for Celestial. I wasn't either. I figured Celestial got what she deserved and had nobody but herself to blame for her humiliation.

Opal rushed down the hall to meet us. She'd taken off her stage makeup, and her face was glowing. "Guess what, Aunt Julia? Miss Barnes says I'm good enough for a summer theater company, and she's going to write a recommendation for me for next year. Isn't that fabulous?"

"That's wonderful, Opal," Aunt Julia said. "Congratulations."

Opal threw her arms around me. "Your scenery is gorgeous! It looked so real, I could almost hear Spoon River running! I'm so happy I'm about to explode."

Sunday plowed through the crowd. "I'm starving! Who's up for burgers and fries?"

"At this hour?" Aunt Julia asked.

"Oh, don't be a stick-in-the-mud," Sunday said. "It's still early. Besides it isn't as if you have a plane to catch." She elbowed Aunt Julia in the ribs. "What do you say? You can give me a ride in that fancy car of yours."

"You are impossible," Aunt Julia said, fishing her car keys from her purse. "Come on, then. Let's go."

We went out to the parking lot and piled into the car, me and Opal in the backseat, Sunday riding shot-gun with Aunt Julia. We cranked the radio up as loud as it would go and sang with Elvis all the way to town.

CHAPTER TWENTY-TWO

Summer hadn't arrived yet, but we could feel it coming, and that made it harder for the teachers to keep our attention. They planned a lot of end-of-school activities that kept us busy without really teaching us anything. Every Monday, Mr. Stanley held a math bee in the cafeteria. He chose four team captains, and they picked the best students for their teams. I didn't mind being picked last. It gave me more time to think about the letter we'd received from Daddy at Easter. Soon he'd be out of the hospital and on his way to get Opal and me the minute school was out. In between reciting the definitions of polygons and acute angles, I thought about how much I'd missed my daddy and my house on Piney Road. I thought about Jean Ann, my so-called best friend, who had not written to me even once the whole time I'd been gone. I wondered whether everything would be the same between us or whether we had changed too much to pick up our friendship where we had left off when Mama yanked me out of Texas.

One day Coach Riley herded us out to the parking lot for a bike safety class, even though half of us didn't own bikes. Picture thirty-two almost-eighth-graders pretending to weave in and out of traffic cones, giving hand signals for turns and stops. Cooley made screeching noises and crashing sounds at the stop signs and made everybody laugh until Coach Riley threatened to send him to the office. Then we went inside to watch a film about bike safety on the road. One thing about Coach Riley: He could find a film to suit any occasion.

Powla was the only one who refused to give us busywork, the only one who made us keep on creating and thinking, filling our minds with so many ideas about art and raising so many questions I thought my head might explode. I never dreamed the best teacher in the school would get in trouble for teaching us to think. But she did, and it was my fault.

The Monday after *Spoon River Anthology,* I took my *American Dreams* piece to school. I'd copied the style of Rivera and Orozco, filling my canvas with figures of people like Mama and Aunt Julia looking up toward their dreams, and with pictures of Cherokees like

Charlie, and black people like the kids in the Louisiana sit-ins, dreaming for the same chances the rest of us got. At the top I painted Uncle Sam in a striped hat, handing a Bill of Rights to some people, but tugging it away from the Indian and the Negroes, to show that it's the powerful people who make the rules the rest of us are supposed to live by. From what I had learned in history class, it seemed that nothing was wrong if certain people wanted to do it. I hoped that when Miss Browning saw it, she'd decide I was finally working up to my full potential.

Powla was stunned when she saw my picture, and I won't kid you, I was pretty pleased with it myself. I could see how much I had improved since the beginning of the year. When Powla showed it to the class, Nathan said, "Wow," under his breath, and after that I didn't care what anyone else thought. I wanted his approval almost as much as I wanted hers. I couldn't help it.

After Miss Browning had seen it, Powla mounted my picture in the art room next to a copy of *Tropical America*. It covered the whole bulletin board. When Principal Conley walked in one morning a few days later, my piece was pretty hard to miss.

Powla was teaching us about Jackson Pollock's action paintings, and we were sprawled on the floor with our paint cans, dribbling color onto canvas in random patterns that looked more like the aftermath of a cafeteria food fight than an actual picture. But we were laughing and having fun, and Powla was on her hands and knees with us when the principal came in with his clipboard, his glasses riding on top of his bald head. Usually when he wanted to talk to Powla, he just opened the door, stuck his head in, and motioned her into the hallway, but today he strode to the middle of the room, looking so full of official business that the whole room went quiet.

He took a look around and his face got all shocked-looking, like he'd just survived a big explosion. He stepped over a bunch of our open paint cans. "What on earth is going on in here?"

Powla stood up and wiped her hands on a paint rag. "This is an art class, sir. We are making art." She smiled. "The process is not always a tidy one."

Principal Conley's eyes locked onto *Tropical America.* He frowned, put on his glasses, and stepped up for a closer look. Then he saw my picture and my signature in the corner, and he totally came unhinged. He spun around. "Is this what you're teaching these kids, Miss Mendez? To glorify disobedience and denigrate our government? This isn't art, it's nothing but Communist propaganda!"

Mr. Conley trained his beady eyes on me. "Garnet Hubbard. You have been a troublemaker from the get-go. Writing disrespectful answers on your math paper, running away from school, causing a near riot at the

Christmas program, and now this. Are you *trying* to get expelled?"

"No, sir," I said. "But you're the one who said school is supposed to teach us to think. *I* think David Siqueiros told the truth when he said art is supposed to educate people so they can fight for what's right."

"Garnet's piece, and Siqueiros's as well, is art as social commentary," Miss Mendez put in, "which in my opinion is the only art worth making."

The principal pointed to our half-finished Pollock painting lying on the floor. "What commentary does this so-called art make?"

Before Powla could answer, he said, "I came to conduct the required evaluation of your teaching, but this is not the appropriate time. When I return, I'll expect to see something more appropriate for impressionable children."

"They are not children. They are young adults quite capable of thinking for themselves."

We all sat up straighter at that, in love with Miss Mendez for taking us seriously.

"Nevertheless," Mr. Conley said. "I insist you forget the Mexican rabble-rousers you seem to be so fond of, and focus on more appropriate subjects." He waved his hand. "Landscapes, self-portraits, still-life studies. Anything but sacrilege and anarchy."

"Painting vases of flowers and bowls of fruit will teach them nothing about life."

"It isn't your job to teach them about life."

"I'm sorry, Mr. Conley, but I disagree."

"Disagree all you want, but as long as you work here, you'll do it my way. Otherwise, you can tell it to the school board."

He stomped out and Powla said softly, "Maybe I will."

We all felt bad for her, but we were also fascinated. I'm pretty sure it was the first time we'd ever seen a principal chewing out one of his own kind.

Powla sighed deeply and glanced at the clock. "The bell is about to ring. Let's get these canvases put away and clean up."

She was trying to act like what had just happened was no big deal, but I could see she was upset. I felt horrible for everything I had put her through, first by skipping her class and running away to Nashville, then by painting something that had made Mr. Conley mad. While everybody was busy putting the lids on the paint cans and stacking the canvases, I said to her, "It's my fault. I'll take my picture down now."

"You will do no such thing."

"Mr. Conley—"

"Can swallow a rotten corncob for all I care." Powla smiled. "If you've learned nothing else all year, Garnet, I hope you've learned that you must be willing to stand up for what you believe, and put it on the canvas. If you can't do that, then you can't be a real artist. This we learned from Diego Rivera, right?"

I nodded. I wasn't the best history student on the planet—just ask Miss Browning—but I had learned enough to know that the struggle for dreams I'd put into my picture was right and true.

"I'm sorry I got you in trouble," I said, as the bell rang and people hurried out.

Powla laughed. "I seem to get into plenty of trouble all by myself. Don't worry about it."

The rest of the week was devoted to cleaning cupboards, washing chalkboards, turning in textbooks, and paying library fines. The school crafts fair was scheduled for the last weekend before the year ended, and I was busy painting pictures to sell in the art gallery. I painted a still life of flowers in a vase, a picture of Black Beauty copied from the cover of my book, and one of Charlie Twelvetrees paddling his canoe on Willow River. Pictures I hoped wouldn't give Mr. Conley a heart attack.

"This is wonderful," Powla said, holding my picture of Charlie to the light.

It was the Friday before the fair, and regular afternoon classes were canceled so everyone could get ready for it. Cooley was helping the home ec teachers set up tables for selling baked goods. Lee Crockett and a couple of other boys from art class were helping the shop teacher set up a display of birdhouses his students had made. Miss Mendez and I were setting up the art gallery. Nathan was helping us put up shelves for the pottery exhibit. He stopped long enough to take a look at my picture of Charlie.

"Garnet's a regular Rembrandt," he said. "I can't draw anything."

"But you're a good ballplayer," I said. It seemed easier to talk to him when Powla was around.

"You still haven't come to a game," Nathan said. "We're playing in Linville on Sunday."

"Maybe I'll come." I tossed my hair the way I'd seen Opal do it.

Nathan's face turned red. He finished setting up the shelves and picked up his glove. "I've got practice. See you."

When the door closed behind him, Powla said, "My, my, Garnet. You played that boy like a violin."

"Ma'am?"

"It's obvious he's got a huge crush on you, so keep him guessing. The harder you are to get, the better boys like it."

"That's exactly what my sister says."

Powla laughed. "Just put Mr. Nathan Brown out of his misery and go to one of his games if you like him."

I felt my face turning red. She pretended not to notice. "Help me hang this watercolor."

We finished hanging the pictures and stood back to admire the final result. I was proud of my work, but Polly Barton's watercolor of the Willow River in winter was better. Faith had made a picture of her daddy's church with an angel watching over it. Cooley's contribution was a lopsided brown vase with white lines etched into it. Some of the eighth graders had made silk-screened pictures; others had made charcoal sketches of houses, fields, animals, and people.

"That should do it." Powla gathered up her stuff and we went to the door. "I'll see you tomorrow."

I rode the bus home. Opal stayed behind to help Cheryl finish setting up the freshman exhibit in the home ec room. Some of the girls had made aprons, pot holders, and cloth purses to sell. Others were bringing brownies, muffins, cakes, and pies. Since Opal had no interest in baking or sewing, she volunteered to set up the exhibit and act as cashier during the fair.

When I got home, Aunt Julia was sitting in the living room listening to her opera recordings. Mozart was curled up at her feet, dreaming his cat dreams.

"Aunt Julia?"

She turned off the music. "Yes?"

"I was wondering. Could you drive me to the ballpark Sunday afternoon? A friend invited me to watch the game."

"A friend? Here in Willow Flats?" Her blue eyes twinkled.

"It's about time, now that school is over."

"No law says you can't come visit me next summer," Aunt Julia said. "I imagine he'll still be around."

"Who said it was a he?" I snagged a couple of cookies off the plate in the kitchen and washed them down with cold milk.

"Do I look like I just fell off a turnip truck? As improbable as it may seem, I was young once. I know a crush when I see one."

"It's just a stupid baseball game."

"Right." Aunt Julia munched on a cookie. "The answer is yes. I will drive you to the ballpark if you'll help me wash my canning jars. Strawberries are coming in and it's time to make jam."

I spent the next two hours kneeling over a tub of scalding hot water, elbow deep in suds, washing jam jars until my fingers wrinkled and my knees ached. Aunt Julia stacked them in boxes and left them in the kitchen. When Opal came home, we ate a late supper on the porch, watching the fireflies lighting up the dark.

Since the incident at the river with Travis, Opal had given up on boys. Most days she came straight home from school to practice her acting techniques up in our room. All she talked about now was next summer, when she would go away to work in a real theater company.

After supper Aunt Julia said, "We got a postcard from your mother today. She has a job singing backup with Jimmy Bowers and the Bluegrass Boys."

"Jimmy Bowers?" Opal asked. "That old guy?

Mama always called him a loser. And she hates blue-grass! I can't believe she'd sing with him." With the toe of her sneaker, Opal set the porch swing in motion. "Then again, who else would hire her?"

It was the truth, but I felt sorry for Mama. Her shining dream was getting farther and farther away, and she was trying desperately to grab ahold of a piece of it wherever she could find it.

"They're going to sing at the fairs this summer," Aunt Julia went on. "Melanie says maybe she'll get to Mirabeau in August."

"Just in time to celebrate her birthday," Opal said wryly. "That's Mama, always thinking of herself."

Which was also true, but somehow my bitterness toward my mother had softened into something less painful. Melanie McClain would never be the mother I wanted, but I couldn't let that fact ruin my life.

Aunt Julia got up from the porch swing. "You two can stay up if you want, but I'm going to bed."

"We'll be in soon," Opal said. "We've got a long day tomorrow."

"And your sister has a date on Sunday afternoon," Aunt Julia said. "Good night, girls."

"A date?" Opal said when Aunt Julia had gone. "How come you didn't tell me?"

"It isn't a real date. Nathan invited me to his ball game, that's all."

"Oh, wow!" Opal jumped up and began to pace.

"We've got only one day to plan your wardrobe. And do your nails. They're a mess with all that paint under them. What about your hair? Up? Or down." She peered into my face. "Up will be cooler, but you definitely look cuter with a little hair around your face. Maybe we could do a ponytail and leave a few strands free."

"Opal, I'll be sitting in the stands and he'll be out on the field. It doesn't matter."

"Of course it matters! You can wear my new yellow shirt and your white shorts. You'll look fabulous!"

We went inside and ran upstairs to our room. Opal took her shirt from the closet. "Here. It's yours."

It was hard not to catch her enthusiasm. I changed into my nightshirt and fell into bed, too full of mixed-up feelings to sleep. All year I had dreamed of cracking the code that would let me into Opal's world of friends and dates and parties. And just as I was starting to fit in, the school year was over. Soon I'd be going back to Mirabeau. Now I wasn't sure where I wanted to be.

The next day we went to the crafts fair at school. People from all over milled in the parking lot and hall-ways, eating brownies and cookies and taking in the exhibits. Aunt Julia and Sunday went around together, admiring the displays of handmade jewelry, quilt squares, and birdhouses. After I helped Powla set out price tags for everything in the art gallery, I sat behind a desk with a cash box and waited for customers. Mrs.

Underwood came with a couple of ladies from her choir. One of them bought Faith's angel picture right away. Mrs. Underwood studied everything before she made up her mind to buy Polly's winter scene. Then she picked up my flower picture and held it out at arm's length. "This will look nice in my powder room," she said. "The colors match my towels."

Powla shot me a wry grin as she wrapped up their purchases. When they had moved off down the stairs, she laughed. "You should have seen your face when Mrs. Underwood said your picture matched her towels. Get used to it, Garnet. Sometimes people buy art for the wrong reasons. But we can't let that stop our work." She rested her hand on my shoulder. "You have a gift, but it's worthless unless you use it. Promise you won't waste it. Promise me you'll find teachers to encourage your talent."

This was beginning to sound like good-bye, and I wasn't ready for it. I picked up Cooley's vase and turned it around in my hands.

"I'm leaving tomorrow," Powla said quietly.

"No! So soon?" My throat closed up.

"Monday's the last day of school and it's an assembly day, so there won't be regular classes. There's no point in prolonging things. I've heard the gossip about how I dress, what I paint, how I live. The school board will never renew my contract. At least I can have the satisfaction of resigning instead of waiting to be dismissed."

"Where will you go?"

She shrugged. "Now that my father is better, I'm considering a trip to Mexico. I have a friend who teaches at a small art institute near San Miguel de Allende. Perhaps I'll teach there. Perhaps I'll go back to Spain." She laughed. "I am not cut out for a place like Willow Flats, Oklahoma."

More people wandered in. A woman wearing a faded T-shirt bought Cooley's vase and one of the silk screens. A white-haired couple peered at each picture in turn before the woman picked up my Black Beauty painting. "I'll take this one. My granddaughter loves horses."

I counted out her change, amazed that people who were not even kin to me were paying real money for my work.

At lunchtime we bought lemonade and chicken salad sandwiches from the home ec girls and ate in the gallery. Powla looked around at the half-empty shelves. "I'd say you've had a very good day. Two of your pieces sold."

I took a long sip of cold lemonade. "Nobody bought my picture of Charlie, though, and it's the best one."

"I think so too. Don't give up. The day isn't over yet."

But hardly anybody came in after lunch, and nobody bought anything. Opal and Cheryl came in, arm in arm, laughing about some boy who had tripped over his own shoelaces and fallen face-first into a chocolate sheet cake. "Talk about a brown nose!" Cheryl giggled. "The whole thing was hysterical."

"I'm sure it was a real scream," Powla said, grinning. "How about helping us pack this stuff up?"

We packed everything except my picture of Charlie into boxes and carried them to the storeroom on the first floor so the owners could claim them on Monday. Then Cheryl and Opal ran outside to talk to Miss Barnes.

"Well," Powla said, looking around, "I guess this is it."

Everything was happening too fast. An empty space opened up inside me. My throat ached. "Miss Mendez," I began, "I . . ."

Powla's dark eyes glittered. "I'm not very good at saying good-bye."

"I don't want you to go," I said.

"But you're going home to Texas very soon, right?" I nodded.

"So in any case, we wouldn't be together next year." She fished a pen from her pocket and took a piece of paper off the storeroom shelf. "Give me your address and I'll send you a postcard once I'm settled somewhere."

Then she removed one of her silver bracelets, a wide one with flowers carved into the edges, and pressed it into my hand. "Here. A little gift to remind you of your promise."

I scribbled my address on Piney Road, shoved the paper into her hands, and ran outside swallowing tears, clutching my bracelet and my picture of Charlie tight against my chest.

"There you are," Aunt Julia said. "Ready to go?"

We got into the car, and I held my picture of Charlie on my lap as we headed home. We passed Charlie's cabin, and the place where he had first given me the worry dolls. Remembering Charlie, I was glad the picture was still mine.

A horn sounded and a gray car passed us, Mr. Conley at the wheel. I was mad at him for what he'd done to Miss Mendez, but I pitied him too, for being so afraid of people whose ideas weren't the same as his own. He could keep Powla from teaching in Willow Flats, but he couldn't stop her from telling the truth. That was the important thing. I thought of the gifts she'd given me that year—a Christmas bauble, a silver bracelet, and a future. I hoped I wouldn't let her down.

After church the next day I changed into Opal's yellow shirt, my white shorts, and a pair of sandals. Opal pulled my hair into a ponytail and did the best she could with my ragged fingernails, then finished off her creation by nearly drowning me in My Sin.

"Stop!" I waved my hand in front of my nose to disperse the fumes.

"You don't want to smell like turpentine, do you?" my sister asked. "Now hold still." She helped me with my Cotton Candy lipstick, and I went downstairs feeling like I belonged to the pretty girls' club at last.

Opal followed me out to the car. "Have fun, okay?"

Aunt Julia drove me to the baseball park and let me off near the front gate. A few girls were already sitting in the bleachers. One of them said, "Hi!" and patted an empty spot beside her. "Sit here if you want."

"Thanks."

"I'm Beth," the girl said. "Do you live in Linville?"

"Willow Flats. Nathan Brown invited me."

"Wow. Nathan. He played in my brother's summer league one year. That boy is so fine!"

Then the teams trotted onto the field and the announcer read the starting lineups. When Nathan's name was called, he looked up into the stands. I waved, but he didn't see me. He picked up his bat and took a few practice swings, and the game started.

As much as I loved baseball, it was hard to keep my mind on the game. I couldn't take my eyes off Nathan, even when he was sitting on the bench. I thought about what I would say to him after the game. I wondered if my ponytail was drooping in the heat, and whether my lipstick had smeared. As the game went on, it got hotter in the bleachers and I started to worry that my deodorant had quit working. I casually raised both arms like I was adjusting my ponytail, and gave my underarms a sniff. They smelled okay.

Almost before I knew it, Willow Flats came to bat

for the last time, trailing 3-2. The first player hit a long ball to right field and sprinted all the way to second base. The next one hit a blooper that put him on first. The third one walked, and Nathan came to the plate with the bases loaded. He pulled his cap low over his eyes and pounded his bat into the dirt.

"Yea, Nathan!" I yelled. "Hit a grand slam! You can do it!"

He looked up into the stands half a second before the first pitch crossed the plate.

Strike one.

Nathan wiped his palms on his uniform, gripped the bat, and crouched over the plate. The second pitch was fast and inside. Nathan swung and missed. The Warriors fans groaned.

Nathan hit the third pitch, but it went foul. Now I was sitting on the edge of the bleachers, holding my breath. "Come on, Nathan. Watch the ball!"

I crossed my fingers and prayed he'd get a hit. But he swung hard at the next pitch and struck out, ending the game. The Linville fans whooped and clapped. A man with a camera around his neck jogged onto the field and took pictures as the teams headed toward the dugouts.

I reached the fence just as Nathan trotted by. "Nathan!"

He looked up. His eyes were red and wet. Seeing how much the loss had hurt him, I felt like crying too.

"You played a great game anyway," I said. "The season's just started. One loss won't matter."

"Leave me alone."

He turned on his heel and walked off the field.

Beth came up behind me just as Aunt Julia pulled into the parking lot. "Don't worry, he'll get over it."

"I have to go."

"Me too. Maybe I'll see you again sometime!" Beth called as I ran for the car.

"How did it go?" Aunt Julia asked.

"We lost." I got in and slammed the door. "Nathan blames me because he struck out."

"Well, that's just ridiculous." We bounced across the dirt parking lot and pulled onto the highway. "How could it possibly be your fault?"

"I don't know! First he keeps pushing me to come to a game, and then when I do he won't even speak to me. I will never understand boys."

"Welcome to the club." Aunt Julia patted my hand. "Don't give Nathan Brown another thought. I have good news. Your daddy called the store this afternoon. He'll be here the day after tomorrow."

CHAPTER TWENTY-THREE

Dreams are funny things. You carry them around for so long they become as much a part of you as breath itself. You walk around with a stomach full of butterflies, waiting for dreams to come true. Then when they do, it's a big letdown because they never turn out the way you imagined.

Ever since Daddy's accident, I'd dreamed of the day he would come to Willow Flats to take me home. Now that the day was almost here, instead of feeling happy, I was worried he had changed, that he wouldn't be the same person who told jokes and taught me to play baseball. I was scared that his homecoming would turn into another big disappointment in a year that had had more than its share of them.

On Monday morning Opal and I got up as usual

and dressed for our very last day of school in Willow
Flats. Since the seventh graders had to participate in a
field day in the afternoon, Mr. Conley had given us
permission to wear shorts to school. I wore a pair of
pink ones handed down from Opal, and a white
blouse. Opal wore a navy skirt and the yellow blouse I'd
worn to Nathan's game.

We had breakfast with Aunt Julia and went out to
wait for the bus. I was so excited to be through with
school at last that I could barely stand still. I couldn't
wait to get away forever from Celestial and Faith and
their snooty friends, from the ninth-grade boys who
hit me with spit wads and made fun of the way I talked,
from Mr. Conley who frowned at me like I was a serial
killer every time he saw me in the hall. But Opal looked
like she was about to cry.

"What's the matter?" I asked. "Don't tell me you're
all broken up over leaving Willow Flats."

"I've made some good friends here," Opal said.
"I'll miss Cheryl and Tacy."

"I won't miss anybody," I said. "Except Miss
Mendez, and she's already gone."

"You'll miss Nathan, I bet."

"Maybe. He won't miss me, though."

"Yes, he will. Boys never tell you how they feel.
We're supposed to be able to look at them and figure
out what they're thinking."

The bus rattled down the road. Sunday braked and

threw the door open. "Hi, girls! Can you believe this year is finally over?"

Me and Opal sat together, and we headed for school. The bus was noisier than ever that day; everybody was excited and ready for summer vacation. Annalee Barton got on the bus wearing a pair of red plastic sunglasses and a sundress with spaghetti straps. She grinned and waved to me as she went past my seat. Celestial Jones got on. Little Miss Perfect sashayed down the aisle and sat with Seth Naylor, the human scarecrow who had been Opal's heartthrob way back last fall. Opal just rolled her eyes when Seth put his arm around Celestial.

Sunday pulled up to the schoolhouse and killed the engine. "This bus is leaving promptly at three o'clock today," she announced. "Don't anybody stay after school or you'll miss it."

We all laughed. Nobody was planning to stay one second past the last bell, and Sunday knew it. She grinned and cranked open the door, and we piled out.

The little kids sprinted to their school across the road. Everyone else headed for the high school auditorium for the awards assembly. Opal went to find her friends, and I sat in the back row by myself. Five minutes after Mr. Conley started handing out plaques, ribbons, and certificates for this and that, I wished I'd brought my sketchbook or a good book to read. I didn't know any of the kids whose names were called, and I was bored stiff.

After the awards were handed out, several of the

teachers made announcements, and Mr. Conley talked
to the seniors about the graduation ceremony planned
for the next Saturday night. Then we were sent to various locations for the rest of the morning. The seniors
left to practice for graduation. The juniors went to a
Class of '62 reception in the gym, hosted by the athletes' moms. The freshmen and sophomores got the
best deal; they stayed in the auditorium to watch a
movie starring Rock Hudson and Doris Day.

Mr. Riley herded all the seventh and eighth graders
onto the football field, where we listened to a bunch of
college kids, boys mostly, talk about the advantages
participating in athletics had given them. Then we
broke up into teams and practiced batting, throwing,
and catching balls. I kept trying to catch Nathan's eye,
to see if I could figure out what was going on in his
head, but he remained a big mystery.

After lunch the high schoolers filled the bleachers,
and the seventh graders provided the entertainment by
participating in a bunch of silly games like sack races, a
water balloon toss, and a three-person relay. I was hoping I'd get paired with Nathan for something, but Mr.
Riley kept the boys and girls separated, and I wound up
running the sack race against Faith Underwood and a
couple of girls from my English class.

When the games were over, Mr. Riley gave us all a
field day participation ribbon and handed out
lemonade to cool us down. The band took the field

and played a few songs I couldn't recognize. Then the choir director motioned us to our feet for the singing of the school song.

> Willow Flats, Willow Flats,
> you're the dearest school to me.
> Willow Flats, Willow Flats,
> we sing praises unto thee.
> When from your doors at last we go,
> we will ever love thee so.
> Oh, to thee we tip our hats,
> dear Wil-low Flats.

I looked up into the bleachers and found Opal standing between Tacy and Cheryl. They had their arms wound around each other's waists and were swaying to the words of the song. I couldn't tell whether Opal was crying, but Tacy's shoulders were shaking, and she was wiping her eyes with every other word, carrying on like she expected to die that night and would never see Opal and Cheryl again.

The choir director waved her arms and shouted into her microphone, "One more time, Warriors! Really sing out this time!"

"Willow Flats," I sang,

> Willow Flats,
> you're the dumbest school to me.

Willow Flats, Willow Flats,
how lame can one place be?
When from your doors today I flee,
you have seen the last of me.
Don't wait for me to tip my hat
to Wil-low Flats.

It's amazing how singing can make a person feel
so great.

Mr. Riley blew his whistle, the final bell rang, and we
stampeded for the buses, yelling and whooping. Opal
caught up with me just before I reached the driveway.

"Tell Aunt Julia I've gone with Cheryl and Tacy to
the drugstore for a Coke, okay?"

"Don't be late," I said. "Daddy's coming tomorrow."

"Do you think I'd forget that?" Opal said.

I climbed on the bus and took my usual seat behind
Sunday. She grinned at me. "Julia says your daddy will
be here tomorrow. I'll bet you're excited."

"Yes, ma'am. It's been nearly a year since I've seen
him. I can't wait to go home."

"Well, don't you go leaving town without saying
good-bye, you hear?"

"I won't. I still owe you twenty dollars."

Sunday laughed. "I'd forgotten all about that."

We talked all the way to Aunt Julia's. When we got
there, Sunday opened the door and said, "See you,
Garnet."

Opal came in before supper. We helped Aunt Julia make chicken salad and iced tea, and afterward we went upstairs to pack. Opal slept like the dead that night, but I couldn't settle down. I hardly slept at all, and the next morning when I heard Aunt Julia banging around in the kitchen, I got up and went down to help her prepare a feast in honor of Daddy's homecoming.

Aunt Julia cooked two kinds of meat, platters of vegetables, a coconut cake, and a lemon meringue pie. Between the chores she assigned to me—beating egg whites and peeling potatoes—I paced back and forth to the window, watching for Daddy's truck.

"Settle down, Garnet," Opal said after my umpteenth trip. She had slept late, then spent an hour fixing her hair. "You're wearing a path in the rug."

"Let her be," Aunt Julia said. "She's just anxious to see her daddy."

"Well, so am I," Opal said. "But a watched pot never boils."

"Garnet, set the table for me," Aunt Julia said. "And don't forget the iced tea spoons."

I was in the kitchen, getting knives and spoons out of the silverware drawer, when the screen door squeaked open and Daddy yelled, "Hey! Anybody home?"

You might expect I would take off like a shot and throw myself into Daddy's arms, but sudden shyness held me back. Opal grabbed my hand, and I saw that she was nervous too. Our fingers weaved together and we went out to see Daddy.

He stood there in a new pair of jeans, his favorite cowboy boots, and a brown striped shirt I remembered from last summer. His hair was cropped short like he'd just joined the Marines, and he wore a black patch over one eye. The skin on his cheek was tight and shiny, like plastic. I smiled, hoping he couldn't see the shock I was feeling inside. Then he grinned. It was a little lopsided, but still it was my daddy's grin. He opened his arms, and my emotions rushed out like water over a dam. I fell into his arms, sobbing.

He wrapped one arm around me and the other one around Opal, and we held on for a long time, taking in his familiar smells of hair tonic and spearmint. Daddy took my face in his hands and brushed away my tears with his thumbs. "Look at you," he said softly. "You grew up while my back was turned. You sure are a sight for sore eyes, Garnet Hubbard." He kissed the top of Opal's head. "You too, princess."

Aunt Julia said, "I prayed for you every night, Duane. I'm glad you're all right."

"I appreciate that, Julia. And everything you've done for the girls."

Aunt Julia looked like she was about to cry, and Daddy's good eye looked wet too. He cleared his throat, cocked his head, and changed the subject

before we all started crying again. "Is it wishful thinking, or do I smell roast beef?"

"Come and see," I said, grateful that Daddy had
lightened our mood.

He laughed his world-famous squinty-eyed
laugh, and I wasn't afraid anymore. Later we would
talk about Mama and how our lives would be different without her, but right then all that mattered was
that I had my daddy back. The fire had altered him
on the outside, but nothing, not even losing Mama,
had changed his heart.

"Hey, girls . . . ," he began as we headed to the din-
ing room.

Opal said, "Come on, Dad. Let's hear it."

Aunt Julia brought the food to the table. Daddy
held her chair for her and we all sat down. Then Daddy
said, "I saw this one at a railroad crossing in Slidell.
'Train approaching, whistle squealing. Pause! Avoid
that run-down feeling.'"

Me and Opal yelled, "Burma Shave!" and Aunt
Julia laughed.

"Pretty funny." Opal spooned mashed potatoes
onto her plate and passed the platter to me. Then she
said, "Guess what, Daddy? Garnet's got a boyfriend."

"A boyfriend?"

"No! Some dumb boy asked me to a baseball game,
and then got mad at me when he struck out. He's not
my boyfriend."

"Thank goodness," Daddy teased. "I'm not up to planning a wedding this year."

He took another bite of roast beef and told us he'd gone by our house on his way to Oklahoma, and everything was just the way we left it. "We may want to paint, change things up. When we get around to it."

"Sure, Dad," Opal said. "I'm ready for a change."

We stayed at the table a long time that day, catching Daddy up on everything that had happened in our lives since last summer. I told him about Powla, about my paintings, and that I hoped to be a real artist someday.

"Maybe you can get a job painting posters for the Mirabeau carnival this summer." Daddy helped himself to a slab of coconut cake.

"Can we go this year, Dad?" Opal asked.

"I'm counting on it," Daddy said. "I love the carnival."

I did too. I loved the clatter of the roller coaster, the sounds of people screaming as it whooshed down, and the rough-voiced men begging you to waste your money to win a cheap prize. I loved filling up on hot dogs and caramel apples, and the sticky feel of cotton candy melting on my tongue.

Aunt Julia got up from the table and brought Daddy the newspaper story about the *Spoon River Anthology*. Opal told him about her chance to join the summer theater company next year and recited her

Constance Hately speech all over again, a private performance just for him.

Daddy took it all in until his good eye began to
droop and he stretched out on the sofa in the living
room for a nap. After Opal and I helped Aunt Julia
clean up the kitchen, Opal went upstairs to read, and I
went out to the garden. Aunt Julia's whirligigs turned
in the breeze, a blur of color against the new green.
The air was full of the smell of summer. Everywhere I
looked, something was blooming—hollyhocks,
marigolds, and rosebushes heavy with buds just waiting
to unfurl.

Mozart came out and crawled into my lap. I stroked
his back and thought about the year that had been both
terrible and wonderful, a year in which I'd realized
that other people's dreams have to matter too, even
when it means letting go of some of your own. Living
with Aunt Julia had taught me that the people who stay
are just as important as the ones who go, and that the
best home of all is the one you make inside yourself.

A white convertible sped past the mailbox, raising a
cloud of dust that hung in the air like powdered gold.
"Hey!" Nathan yelled as the car hurtled past. "Hey,
Garnet!"

Nathan raised his arm and waved. I waved back.

AUTHOR'S NOTE

As a young girl coming of age in the 1960s, I experienced firsthand many of the societal changes I write about in this novel, including the beginnings of the civil rights movement; the birth of space exploration; and the fear of Communism that deepened in the wake of Russia's launch of its Sputnik satellites, the Communist convention held in New York, and the downing of an American spy plane over Russia.

Like adolescence itself, the 1960s held both great promise and great uncertainty. Across the South, Dr. Martin Luther King Jr. was leading sit-ins and protest marches, calling attention to the injustices affecting black Americans, encouraging profound change in the social order of the country. While black athletes were winning medals at the 1960 Olympics in Rome, ten people, eight of them black, were shot in a race riot on a beach in Biloxi, Mississippi. Senator John F. Kennedy was elected America's first Catholic president and challenged America to put a man on the moon within ten years, a challenge that sparked renewed interest in science and opened outer space as a new frontier for exploration. It was a time of confusion and fear mixed with excitement and hope.

As these events unfolded, I formed opinions about the differences between what I was learning in school and what was happening in the real world, opinions I expressed through writing stories and poems, much as Garnet expresses her thoughts through her *American Dreams* painting.

The Mexican muralists David Siqueiros and Diego Rivera, whom Garnet studies and copies in her own work, are considered by many art scholars to be the most influential muralists of their time. Both used their work to express their political beliefs, beliefs that landed them in trouble with their patrons and with the authorities.

David Siqueiros was a devoted Communist who was imprisoned more than once for his political views. In 1941 he was denied entry into the United States because of a new law that prevented Communists from entering the country. The story of his mural *American Tropical (Tropical America)* is a story of politics, art, and censorship. In the 1930s he came to Los Angeles, California, and was commissioned to paint a mural at the Plaza Art Center, in a part of town heavily populated by poor Mexican immigrants who often lived in deplorable conditions. Moved by the plight of the immigrants, Siqueiros used his art to attack American imperialism.

Using shocking symbols, such as a Mexican Indian on a cross and a worker armed with a gun, as the centerpiece of his mural, Siqueiros hoped to call attention to the injustices suffered by poor workers everywhere. Years later he wrote that "the Mexican hero is rooted in history as a symbol of the oppressed peoples of the world."

His patrons, who had envisioned a mural depicting placid scenes of Mexicans going about their daily lives, were outraged. The work was so controversial that portions of it were painted over within a year of its completion. Within ten years, *American Tropical* was completely erased.

During the 1960s, as the struggle for civil rights continued and the Vietnam War polarized the country, Siqueiros's lost work served as the prototype for murals of protest that appeared in city neighborhoods across the country. In 1988 the Getty Conservation Institute formed a partnership with the City of Los Angeles to conserve *American Tropical*. Since then, conservators have conducted analyses of the paint Siqueiros used, installed an environmental monitoring station, and made digital photographs of the mural's surface. Perhaps someday this important work will be on view once more.

Like Siqueiros, Diego Rivera encouraged revolution both in political life and in art. In 1931 the American philanthropist John D. Rockefeller, who had long admired Rivera's work, commissioned the artist to paint a mural at Rockefeller Center to be called *Man at the Crossroads Looking with Hope and High Vision to the Choosing of a New and Better Future*. Rockefeller hoped the mural would "persuade people to stop and think, above all to stimulate a spiritual awakening." However, once Rivera began work on the mural, he veered from his original plan and included a portrait of Vladimir Lenin, the Russian revolutionary who founded Bolshevism, led the Russian Revolution, and later became head of government. When word got out that Mr. Rockefeller had commissioned a mural containing communist demonstrations, he wrote to Diego Rivera, asking him to "substitute the face of some unknown man where Lenin's face now appears."

In his reply to Rockefeller, Rivera refused, stating he would rather see the entire mural destroyed than change it. Rockefeller then ordered Rivera to stop work on the mural. It was covered over with a canvas, and later the nearly finished mural was chipped off the wall. Upon his return to Mexico, Rivera recreated the mural in the Palace of Fine Arts in Mexico City.

As Garnet explains to Principal Conley, the muralists believed that the purpose of art is to educate people and thus inspire them to fight for liberty, justice, and identity.

For further reading about the muralists and their work, I recommend Desmond Rochfort's *Mexican Muralists: Orozco, Rivera, Siqueiros,* and *Dreaming with His Eyes Open: A Life of Diego Rivera* by Patrick Marnham.

Here's a look at D. Anne Love's next novel,
***Picture Perfect*—available now!**

Now it was June. School was out for the summer and Mama was still gone, still running around all over the country teaching other women how easy it was to Bee Beautiful.

There wasn't much to do in the summer in Eden, Texas. Zane and I planned to spend our vacation driving around in the ten-year-old Ford my daddy the judge had given Zane for his sixteenth birthday, swimming at the lake, and just hanging out while we waited to grow up so our real lives could begin.

Daddy spent most of his time downtown in his courtroom, where he had developed a reputation for sorting out all kinds of disagreements. People said that no matter how complicated and messy a case became, Sumner Trask could think on it and figure out what should be done to make things right. But when his wife went AWOL, leaving him to deal with two teenagers all by himself, he was at a total loss. I guess it's always easier to fix other people's problems than your own.

It was a hot Saturday and I was home alone. Daddy was playing golf with a couple of lawyers, and Zane was down at Threadgill's Garage, supposedly repairing the dents in the Ford, but I suspected it was mostly to hang out with Mr. Threadgill's daughter, Ginger. She was in Zane's class at school and had been our neighbor until last year, when her daddy moved them to a house out on the Dallas highway to be closer to the garage. Ginger was a strawberry blonde, not fat, but not thin, either. I guess you'd say she was solid. Zane said she could fix a flat tire without even breaking a sweat and was the only girl he knew who could explain rack and pinion steering, or tell the difference between a socket wrench and a screwdriver.

I made myself a glass of iced tea and took it out to the porch. The full weight of summer in Eden was settling in; cicadas whirred in the trees, the air was heavy and still. Normally I loved summer, but this year, with Mama Lord-knew-where, Shyla consumed with her prelaw summer school classes, and Lauren Braithwaite, who had been my best friend since third grade, living in Atlanta because her dad had taken a new job there, I was left to face the entire summer without anyone who understood what it was like to be a fourteen-year-old girl.

A black car pulled into the driveway of the vacant house next door, where our elderly neighbor, Mrs. Archer, had lived until she broke her hip and had to go

stay with her daughter in Houston. Now there was a
FOR SALE sign in the weedy yard, and I'd made a habit
of checking out the potential buyers. I watched as a
real estate saleslady ushered her client up the front
steps and unlocked the door. I was ready for something exciting to happen. I hoped that whoever moved
into Mrs. Archer's house would shake things up and
change my life.

Be careful what you wish for.

Growing up
with McElderry Books

Solving Zoe
By Barbara Dee

Sand Dollar Summer
By Kimberly K. Jones

Forever Rose
By Hilary McKay

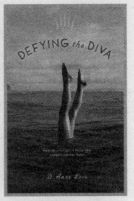

The Blind Faith Hotel
By Pamela Todd

The Genie Scheme
By Kimberly K. Jones

Defying the Diva
By D. Anne Love

 Margaret K. McElderry Books Published by Simon & Schuster

For fun. For inspiration. For you.
Atheneum.

The Secret Language of Girls
by Frances O'Roark Dowell

Kira-Kira
by Cynthia Kadohata

The Higher Power of Lucky
by Susan Patron

Beneath My Mother's Feet
by Amjed Qamar

Standing for Socks
by Elissa Brent Weissman

Here's How I See It—
Here's How It Is
by Heather Henson

Atheneum Books for Young Readers ✱ Published by Simon & Schuster

Read more about girls like you!

The Mother-Daughter
Book Club
by Heather Vogel Frederick

I Wanna Be Your
Shoebox
by Cristina García

The Truth About My
Bat Mitzvah
by Nora Raleigh Baskin

The Teashop Girls
by Laura Schaefer

My So-Called Family
by Courtney Sheinmel

Published by Simon & Schuster Books for Young Readers
KIDS.simonandschuster.com